Suddenl[y]
Tucker'[s]

"Hang on!" he shouted. A black van zoomed so close it filled the rearview mirror.

Sarah screamed as it smashed their Bronco, pushing them forward. Onyx yelped, his harness holding him fast. Tucker's cell thudded to the floorboard as their vehicle recoiled.

Orange road cones flew up in the air like a bowling ball crashing into pins as the Bronco's front fender smashed into them. Tucker forced the SUV back in the lane, then accelerated until their surroundings were a dark blur.

He veered left as the van closed in on them again, clipping his bumper and throwing off the Bronco's momentum. Sarah gripped the console with both hands, her breath coming in gasps. Holding the SUV steady, Tucker edged away from the concrete wall, his mind whirling in a million directions like the cones he'd struck.

The minivan appeared to be a turbo engine, because he couldn't shake them. If he didn't get away from it soon, they wouldn't survive this situation...

Kerry Johnson is an award-winning author who has been conversing with fictional characters and devouring books since her childhood in the Connecticut woods. A longtime member of American Christian Fiction Writers, she lives on the sunny, stormy west coast of Florida with her husband, two sons, her niece and way too many books. She loves Jesus, long walks, all creatures great and small, and a hot cup of tea all hours of the day.

Books by Kerry Johnson

Love Inspired Suspense

Snowstorm Sabotage
Tunnel Creek Ambush
Christmas Forest Ambush
Hidden Mountain Secrets
Hunted in the Forest
Abducted in the Woods

Visit the Author Profile page at LoveInspired.com.

ABDUCTED IN THE WOODS

KERRY JOHNSON

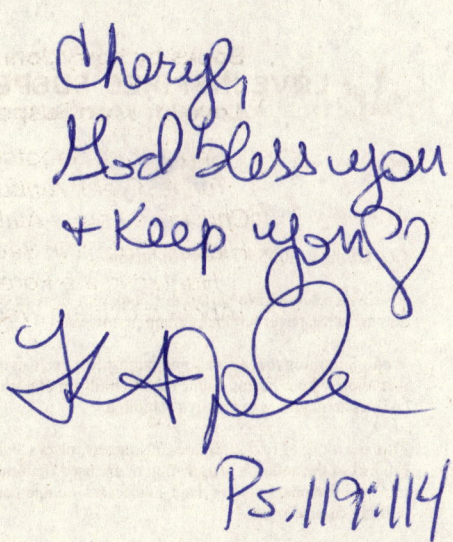

Cheryl,
God Bless you
+ Keep you

Ps. 119:114

If you purchased this book without a cover you should be aware that this book is stolen property. It was reported as "unsold and destroyed" to the publisher, and neither the author nor the publisher has received any payment for this "stripped book."

 **LOVE INSPIRED® SUSPENSE**
INSPIRATIONAL ROMANCE

ISBN-13: 978-1-335-95743-6

Recycling programs for this product may not exist in your area.

Abducted in the Woods

Copyright © 2025 by Kerry Johnson

All rights reserved. No part of this book may be used or reproduced in any manner whatsoever without written permission.

Without limiting the author's and publisher's exclusive rights, any unauthorized use of this publication to train generative artificial intelligence (AI) technologies is expressly prohibited.

This is a work of fiction. Names, characters, places and incidents are either the product of the author's imagination or are used fictitiously. Any resemblance to actual persons, living or dead, businesses, companies, events or locales is entirely coincidental.

For questions and comments about the quality of this book, please contact us at CustomerService@Harlequin.com.

® is a trademark of Harlequin Enterprises ULC.

Love Inspired
22 Adelaide St. West, 41st Floor
Toronto, Ontario M5H 4E3, Canada
www.LoveInspired.com

MIX
Paper | Supporting responsible forestry
FSC® C021394

Printed in Lithuania

Come now, and let us reason together,
saith the Lord: though your sins be as scarlet,
they shall be as white as snow.
—*Isaiah* 1:18

For Cole, Chase and Abbie, our gifts from God. Thanks for putting up with me embarrassing you and for being the coolest young people I know. I cannot wait to see where the Lord leads you three in life. And for those who haven't known a parent's unconditional love—you are created, loved and valued by the Maker of the stars.

ONE

Sarah Brindley couldn't catch her breath.

Not since she'd arrived at her aunt Beverly's cottage. Not since she'd thrown her and her son, Liam's, clothes into her old swim bag and raced away from their home in Fountain View that afternoon. And most definitely not since she saw her husband, Tanner, crumple forward in his office at Zeta Pharmaceuticals with a gunshot wound to his head from two strange men lurking in his office.

She swayed, groping for the kitchen counter.

Despite the quiet atmosphere of the cottage, she could still hear the muted *whomp* of the bullet and the murderous resolve in the shooters' voices as they muttered to each other. She had darted from the elevator and slipped below the empty receptionist's desk, gasping for air like she'd just swam the fifty-free in under twenty-four seconds. With her arms wrapped around her folded legs, she had struggled to comprehend what she'd just witnessed while fervently hoping the two men hadn't seen her or heard the *ding* of the elevator.

Tears had blurred her vision, but the dangerous finality of that horrible moment had been crystal clear. *Tanner was dead.* Despite their marriage floundering, despite his betrayal, she never wanted harm to come upon him.

He had been in his office on a weekend, which wasn't unusual, but that meant few people were around. *No other eyewitnesses*. The cameras. Maybe the security cameras had caught the men in the act.

"I'm hungry, Mommy," Liam called from the cottage's second bedroom. "Can I have some chips?"

"You've had enough chips. How about a sandwich?" Her seven-year-old son was growing like a proverbial weed. She'd thrown a jar of peanut butter and a loaf of bread into her bag while packing for Holloway for just this reason.

After locating a butter knife, she spread peanut butter across two slices of wheat bread, pressed them together and set the sandwich on one of Aunt Bev's white Corelle plates, then grabbed a mini bottled water.

Liam sprawled on his stomach on the guest bed, his tablet flashing and beeping as he played a game. She sank down beside him, the plate held out in her shaky hands. Normally, she didn't allow eating in the bedroom or this much game time, but because of what happened earlier today, *normal* had gone out the window. After driving away in a daze from Tanner's workplace, she had called her friend Amy's husband, Fountain View police officer Drew Stevens, to report Tanner's murder.

Let me take care of it, Sarah, Drew had told her as they spoke on the phone while she drove home. *I'll send officers to Tanner's work, and I'll meet you at your house. Did the suspects see you? Could you identify them?*

I don't think so. I waited until after they left. I think they went down the stairwell, because I heard the door close after I hid under the desk.

And when you left the building, was the parking lot empty? Drew had asked patiently, giving her time in between sobs. *Other than Tanner's car?*

The car in front of her had slammed on their brakes, and

she'd nearly rear-ended them. *I don't remember. I need my son, Drew. But I don't want to stay in our house.*

Listen, once I get your statement, why don't you go somewhere safe. Can you stay with Tanner's mom?

I d-don't know. Sharlene has had so many health issues. I hate to spring this all on her...along with her son's death. For now...can we hold off on telling her? Tanner's brother Tucker might want to do it. Tucker's kind face and bright blue eyes had flashed through her mind. *Liam and I could go up to my aunt's place for a couple days.*

Aunt Beverly's cottage tucked between towering pines and stately oaks on the banks of the Allegheny River. Holloway, Pennsylvania, situated just outside Allegheny National Forest, was the only place Sarah had ever truly felt safe.

Okay, Drew had responded. *We can interview you on the phone or you can come back in a few days once the investigation is underway.*

"Thanks." Liam lifted the sandwich off the plate and wolfed half of it down, bringing the mad rush of her thoughts to a standstill.

"Son, slow down. Chew your food. Remember, your stomach—"

"'My stomach doesn't have teeth,'" he parroted, then made a funny face. "Why does it smell like old dirty socks in here?"

Because the thousand-square-foot cottage hadn't been opened in the last three years. When Aunt Beverly passed away a few years ago, Sarah had been surprised and pleased that her mom's older half-sister had left her the cottage. While Tanner had grumbled about paying the property taxes, she'd been grateful to keep the cozy cottage that held some of her best childhood memories. The interior was still decorated in pastel green and peach from the '90s, which comforted her. Right now, she needed familiar. Needed a place to hide, to process what happened to Tanner and figure out how to tell her son about his dad's death.

Sarah leaned across the bed to muss Liam's spiky blondish-brown hair. One thing was for sure: Now wasn't the time.

"This is an old place, honey. It was built fifty or sixty years ago. I came here as a kid a few times too." When her mom had abandoned her or been on a drinking binge and Aunt Beverly stepped in to fill the gap. "Tomorrow we'll open the windows, and it'll smell better." Holloway was a couple hours' north of Fountain View, and the air here held a deep, clean, brisk quality that Fountain View, a suburb of Philadelphia, didn't have.

"But what about the Christmas tree? We don't have one now." He finished the last bite of his sandwich, and she took his plate.

"Maybe we can find a small one tomorrow. Right now..." She pictured Tanner's face when the men shot him, the shock and horror mirroring her own, and it took all her willpower not to crumble. But she couldn't fall apart in front of her son.

"Mom, are you okay?"

She swallowed the painful knot of emotion in her throat and schooled her features. "I'm just tired, baby."

"Mr. Meow is glad he's not in the car anymore." Liam curled around the huge gray-striped cat, reclining regally on the foot of the bed as though they were in a five-star hotel. Only Mr. Meow could appear nonchalant when their whole world had been turned upside down.

"He's happy wherever you are." She stroked the cat, hoping Liam wouldn't notice how much her hand trembled. Mr. Meow regarded her with those fathomless aquamarine eyes and a soft purr. Liam had struggled with bad dreams and anxiety lately, and she was grateful his counselor had recommended a cat. Though he couldn't take Mr. Meow to school,

Liam loved that the friendly feline always greeted him at the door when he returned home.

Tanner wanted to prescribe medication for Liam, which she'd balked at.

She and Tanner struggled to find common ground in their eight-year marriage, especially after what she'd discovered last year about his indiscretion. Sarah wilted. When they were first married, her Olympic endorsements paid for Tanner's college education, and after she retired from competition at age twenty-three, she'd begun a swim-lesson business while he earned his master's degree. Once out of college, Tanner had been hired by Zeta Pharmaceuticals and worked his way up.

The summer she met him, she'd just turned twenty and had come to train at an aquatic facility in Erie, Pennsylvania, about thirty minutes from Holloway. During the weekends, she'd stayed at the cottage with Aunt Bev. It was here that she'd met outgoing, charismatic Tanner Brindley and his fraternal twin, Tucker.

She pictured the dark-haired, blue-eyed young man who'd helped pull her kayak from the Bent Creek flats during that sudden thunderstorm. She'd been soaking wet and scared, her phone lost in the river. Then Tucker had appeared as if there were no storm and they weren't dodging lightning bolts and rain. He had hefted her kayak and motioned for her to follow him out of the creek area and up the bank, then taken her to safety at his mom's house.

"Can I play some more? I need more chickens for my farm," Liam pleaded, his cheek pressed into Mr. Meow's fur.

"Ten minutes." She kissed her son's head. "I'm going to unpack and check the cabinets. Then it's teeth brushing and bedtime."

Thirty minutes later, with Liam showered, tucked in, and the lights out in the guest bedroom, Sarah settled in the rocking chair on the front porch. Stars winked from the dark expanse of sky. While it had been a mild winter so far, the temperature was forecast to drop the next few days leading up to Christmas. She wrapped her arms across her middle and rocked slowly.

Amy had texted just as Sarah put her phone on the charger in the kitchen, passing on a message from Drew that Tanner's body had been taken to the morgue, they'd dusted the office for prints, and that Drew would be in touch tomorrow. He'd asked again if she wanted to contact Sharlene, Tanner and Tucker's mom, but she preferred to talk to Tucker first.

Sarah caught her lip between her teeth. She'd barely spoken to Tucker the last few years, and now she had to deliver this awful news. She rested her head on the rocking chair's top rail and closed her eyes against another wave of tears.

She should've asked Tucker to meet her here so she could break the news in person.

The wind whistled through the trees, and far away, an owl hooted. She opened her eyes and gazed around the shadowy yard. The solitude of the cottage, initially a welcome reprieve from Fountain View, sent a chill down her jean-clad legs.

A twig cracked in the woods to her left. Sarah uncrossed her arms and leaned forward, her heart galloping. She'd turned off most of the interior lights and parked her SUV in the garage behind the cottage.

Maybe it was just a deer.

Another twig snapped. Her muscles turned to ice, and her thoughts flew to Liam, asleep in the cottage. She peered back at the large front window, then gasped. Mr. Meow stood on his hind legs, front paws to the glass, his luminous eyes focused on the woods to her left.

Had Tanner's murderers seen her earlier and followed them to Holloway?

Please, God. No.

A man materialized from the woods, his large, unmistakable form breaking from the shadows and coming to life before her eyes. He headed for her, his stride slow and methodical. Adrenaline inundated her bloodstream like scalding water, and she jumped to her feet as the life-preserving urge to flee filled every cell of her body. But Liam... She couldn't leave her son alone.

The stranger stalked across the yard until he stood in front of the porch like a specter brought to life.

"I just called the police," Sarah pushed the words out through her bone-dry mouth as she backed up to the door. She needed her phone. "They'll be here any minute." Would he call her bluff?

A crooked grin pushed up his five o'clock shadow. "They won't be here in time, Sarah." Then he lunged up the porch steps. She screamed and swerved away, vaulting the railing. The hard landing jarred her spine, and pain spiderwebbed through her ribs.

She bolted across the small front yard, panic welling in her chest. Instinct told her to get him away from the cottage. Away from Liam.

He followed, thudding down the steps, only a few feet behind her. She shot toward the road, where twin headlights lit up the ground, but he reached her easily. His hands landed on her shoulders like tentacles, grabbing and squeezing. She sidestepped and ducked away, yelping as his nails scored her skin. He wouldn't release her sweatshirt, instead regaining his iron grip on the thick material. Then he shoved her to the ground on the roadside and stood over her, leering like she was a bug and he was about to squash her.

"Mommy?" Liam's voice broke her fearful haze, carrying over from the cottage door.

No, Liam. Stay inside, she wanted to shout. Instead, she wriggled onto her back, situating her hips to kick her attacker's groin. Years of training in the pool, lifting weights and running had paid off. The kick landed square, and he moaned, bending forward, collapsing to the earth beside her. Sarah sprang upright and darted toward the cottage. Liam gaped from the open door, clutching Mr. Meow like a shield. She had to keep him safe. Keep him with her.

She wouldn't leave him alone.

Not like her mom did to her.

"Get inside!" she shouted and gestured as she ran.

"Who is that?" he asked in a high-pitched voice as she took the porch steps in one leap.

"I want you to go inside and hide— Oof!" The attacker's fingers dug into her shoulders, yanking her backward. Pain exploded in her arm sockets as she was wrenched away from Liam and sent flying over the porch railing. "Liam—*no*!"

"Mommy!"

She landed atop one of the azalea bushes in front of the porch. Its branches scratched her neck and poked through her shirt, and pain lightninged up her spine as she struggled out of it and upright.

"Hey, get off me! Let me go!"

Liam's voice rang through the yard, and the world spun as she searched for him. Her breath roared in her chest as the car she'd seen moments ago sped up, blocking the cottage driveway.

"*Liam!* Don't touch my son!" She sprinted toward the car, her slippers sliding on the damp grass.

Her attacker opened the back driver-side door, threw Liam inside and slapped the door shut. Then he raced around to the front-passenger side and dove in.

No. No. *No!*

Her life flashed before her eyes. Her difficult childhood. Abandonment. Abuse at the hands of the men her mom had brought home. The pool, a peaceful refuge with its calming scent of chlorine and familiar sights and sounds. Swimming laps had saved her life. Then Tanner...and Tucker. Her marriage to Tanner and the golden day Liam was born.

Tanner was gone, and she would have to deal with the emotions about that loss. But Liam was her everything. Her whole entire life in one small person who'd taught her how to love. Truly love.

She couldn't lose him.

Hands fisted, nails digging into her palms, she leapt at the accelerating car. Aiming for the front hood, she missed, instead bumping into the side mirror as she grappled for the driver-side door handle. The vehicle's rising speed sent her spinning, and the world careened around her.

The last thing she remembered before the darkness swallowed her was tears streaking her cheeks, dripping onto her neck, then landing on the cold, hard asphalt.

Liam.

Tucker Brindley was too sentimental for his own good. Driving down this road tended to bring out heartache instead of happy memories. Memories of that summer long ago, when he and Tanner weren't fighting as much, when they'd spent hours canoeing and kayaking on the river and in the woods, then when they'd volunteered for the US Forest Service doing tours and forest cleanup. It had been his first taste of life as a forest ranger, and he'd been hooked.

They'd also met Sarah, and she changed their lives forever.

Tucker shook off the reverie and ground the steering wheel between his palms. That was all in the past. He was out here along the river for other reasons. Henry Rodgers had asked him to check on his cabin along the Allegheny River, to make sure nothing was out of place while he and Gertie visited their family in Florida for Christmas. Henry had been good friends with Tucker's dad and was a kindly veteran who still looked out for the Brindley family.

He had jumped at the chance to pay back the older gentleman.

Headlights materialized around the bend, lighting up the forest and coming at him fast. He slowed and hugged the narrow right shoulder, scowling. The other car blew past, shaking his Bronco in its wake, traveling at least twenty over the thirty-five-mph speed limit. An older-model, dark blue or brown Camry. What was their hurry this time of the night? He glanced in his rearview mirror. Too dark to check plates. Onyx whined in the back seat, and Tucker reached back to scratch the dog's favorite spot on his neck, just below his collared harness.

He ascended a hill and drove the last stretch toward Henry's place, Sarah still ruling his thoughts. What were she and Tanner doing this Christmas? His nephew, Liam, was six. No, seven. Unfortunately, Tucker had met him only a couple of times when Liam was little.

Sarah. When she married Tanner several years ago, Tucker attended the wedding. Of course, he had. Despite his bruised heart and his misgivings about Tanner's devotion to Sarah the person, not Sarah the revered Olympian, Tucker needed to be there for them both.

He'd kept the fact that he was in love with the bride quiet, of course.

"Pretty pathetic, aren't I?" Tucker glanced at Onyx.

The sleek black Belgian Malinois whined from his harness in the back seat. Onyx was a new member of the US Forest Service team based out of Holloway. Onyx's handler had been killed in a car accident, and Heath Calhoun, one of Tucker's best friends and a Holloway police officer, had asked Tucker if he wanted to employ the K9 here in Allegheny National Forest since the dog was trained in patrol, narcotics detection and tracking.

After what had happened last year with the cybercriminals coming after Molly, Heath's sister, and her fiancée, FBI agent Eli Buchanan, Onyx would be a great addition to the ranger team.

Tucker slowed as he neared the Rodgers' place. Sarah's aunt Beverly's cottage sat a few hundred yards before Henry's cabin, and driving by always made his chest hitch.

Onyx yapped, straining against his harness, and Tucker slammed on the brakes. What was that? With no streetlights, it was difficult to see the property, but there was no mistaking that something was in the road. A large lump lay near the river side. A deer? No, it wasn't shaped like a deer. More like…a person.

Tucker clenched his jaw. Had the speeding vehicle hit someone out walking in the dark?

"Easy boy." Tucker reached across the dash and snatched his weapon from the glove compartment, slipping it in his waistband. Then he put his Bronco in reverse and parked, leaving space for authorities to get to the person. He leashed Onyx, grabbed his flashlight and then climbed out with the dog. Onyx beelined for the person. In the darkness, long, light hair fanned out and jean-clad legs curled in the fetal position. A woman?

His stomach twisted.

Tucker crouched beside her, gently touching her arm. The woman moaned and rolled onto her back, eyes wide, and Tucker inhaled as if he'd been sucker punched.

"Sarah? It's Tucker." He motioned at the dog. "This is Onyx. What happened? Were you struck by a car?"

She covered her face with her hands and sobbed a name he couldn't quite catch.

"What is it? I need to know what happened."

"It's Liam." She dropped her arms then scrambled up, her legs so unsteady he reached out and cupped one of her elbows. "He's gone. They kidnapped him. Please, you have to call the police."

"I will. But what happened? *Who* took Liam?"

"A man came after me in the front yard... I tried to get him away from the c-cottage, but Liam came out." Her words caught on a sob. "He grabbed him and then drove off in a car with someone else. Please. We have to find him."

She pushed off Tucker and started toward the cottage but stumbled and almost went down again.

"Sarah." He caught up to her then linked her arm with his, shouldering a portion of her weight. Onyx circled beside him, eager to work after sensing Tucker's heightened emotion.

Liam was gone. His brother's son—his nephew—had been *kidnapped*?

Tanner had rarely returned to Holloway after they married and moved away. Once Tucker had seen them when Tanner and Sarah brought Liam to Holloway as a toddler, but it had been a brief visit because it was fire season and Tucker was working long hours in the forest clearing dead brush. Plus, seeing Sarah and Tanner together was never high on his list of priorities. More like *things to avoid*.

Where was Tanner now? He urged her toward the cottage. "How many men were here?"

"Two. A driver and the man who attacked me." She stared up at the heavens as though pleading with God. "Please, we need to find him."

"Any ideas why they came after Liam?"

"There were these men at T-Tanner's office—" She stopped in the front yard and let out a strangled gasp. "Oh, Tucker, I'm so sorry. I should've called you right away. Tanner was... he was killed."

He recoiled. "What...how?" Everything spun around him, and suddenly he needed her to help him stand as much as she needed him.

"He was killed in his office earlier today."

Tucker flinched again, his muscles turning to concrete. Tanner was *dead*? He moved toward the porch steps with robotic motions as her words sank in.

"Does my mom know?"

She shook her head. "I haven't told her yet. I asked Drew—my friend's police officer husband—to wait. I was going to call you tomorrow. I'm sorry, I..."

"It's okay." His thoughts scattered like windblown snowflakes. He understood. Mom was fragile—health problems, according to his aunt Nell, her sister who visited his mom often. He would work out how best to tell her later. Right now, he had to figure out what happened to Liam. Find him. Make sure his nephew was safe.

Tucker steered Sarah up the steps, Onyx on one side of him and Sarah leaning on the other. He held his weapon in one hand and surveyed the aged-wood-and-stone cottage. A rocking chair lay sideways on the front porch, and the front door sat open.

Sarah stopped short. "I think Liam was holding Mr. Meow when they took him."

"That's a cat, I take it?"

"Yes, Liam's cat. They're very attached to each other."

"We'll find them. First, let's get inside. I need to call this in." Tucker ushered them through the door, shut and locked it, then dialed 9-1-1. A dispatcher answered, and Tucker gave a brief description of the night's events as he understood them, shared a detailed description of the Camry he'd seen fly past his Bronco, then he requested officers to come out to Old Forge Road. He hung up and treaded around the cottage, checking window locks and making sure closets were empty. When he returned, Sarah was sitting at the kitchen table, her head in her hands, fingers sunk deep in her hair.

She was still slim and strong, her blond hair longer and darker, framing her hazel eyes set under slender, arched brows. Her athletic build attested to what he'd heard from his mom through the years—Sarah ran a swim-lesson business for children, coached a swim team, and still competed in masters swimming events.

"The police have been notified. They put out an APB on the car. Officers are on their way here, and local and state law enforcement will be on the lookout."

"Thank you," Sarah replied softly.

He angled his head to catch her whispered words.

Tucker's hearing loss had been a source of shame since the car accident all those years ago. The pressure from his head hitting the passenger side window had damaged his right ear drum, taking 40 % of his hearing. No one knew—not even their mom—that the accident had been Tanner's fault. His fraternal twin had been spinning donuts too close to some trees, and while Tanner hadn't been hurt in the ensuing crash, Tucker's perforated ear drum had never fully healed.

He located a notepad and pen in a kitchen drawer, then sat down. "Can you tell me what happened to Tanner first, and then to Liam?"

She shrank under the kitchen light's glare. "When I got out of the elevator at his work, I could see down the hall. His office is at the end, and it's mostly glass. He used to complain about the lack of privacy, which is partly why he often went into work on weekends. Today these two men were standing in front of Tanner's desk. They were well-dressed and—"

"What were they wearing?"

She scrunched up her nose in thought. "Black slacks and dark shirts, I think. I heard raised voices as soon as the elevator door opened, then I saw them. Then one..." She sniffled. "One of the men shot him. They must not have heard the elevator open, but it would've made more noise if I tried to get back on. So, I ran to the receptionist desk near the elevator to hide."

"Did they see you?"

"I don't think so, but by the time I left the building and got in my car, I wasn't paying attention."

Then she recounted the last half-an-hour at the cottage, her voice cracking as she spoke. Her fingers twined in knots on the table, and by the end, her eyes were wide and her breathing erratic.

"Hey, take some slow, deep breaths for me. In and out. There you go. Good." He was bursting with more questions but now wasn't the time. Simple was best. "Today is Saturday. Why was Tanner at work on the weekend?"

"He works weekends all the time. Privacy and quiet, like I said." Her brows sank and her mouth curled down, making her look so sad that he reached out, patting her arm. "And he had a deadline at work—well, the production team did."

"He's no longer selling pharmaceutical products?"

"No. He began overseeing product production in Zeta's laboratory a couple years ago. He was given the supervisory position for a groundbreaking new Parkinson's drug, and he's been working most of the last month as the clinical trials wrapped up."

"I didn't realize he was working on that. Our mom hasn't

mentioned it either." His stomach clenched at the reminder he'd have to call Mom and tell her the terrible news.

She released her hands and crossed her arms over her middle. "I can't help but wonder if his...if what happened today had something to do with that new drug."

"The Parkinson's one?"

She nodded. "I think there were problems in the clinical trials. Adverse reactions, maybe? When things stalled, he was under a great deal of stress. There was a lot of pressure to get it out on the market as soon as possible."

Tucker rubbed his neck. "I'm sorry to ask this but are you sure..." He let the question trail off, partly for her and partly for himself. *Tanner was dead.* The statement still didn't make sense. There was no love lost between him and his brother. Tanner had been arrogant at times and highly competitive. Self-centered and attention-seeking. They'd grown apart as they got older, especially after the car accident, and even more when Sarah came into their lives.

But Tucker had never wished his brother harm. In fact, he'd prayed Tanner would find the Lord.

"If you're asking if he's really dead, the answer is yes. They shot him here." She touched her forehead. "Isn't that...?"

"Fatal? Yes." Tucker released a hard breath and set the pen down. "Alright. That's enough questions for now. When the officers get here, you might have to give your statement once more for—"

Onyx lifted his head and growled a split second before a shadow crossed the cottage's front window.

"Get down!" Tucker sprang at Sarah, knocking them both backward in her chair. He snaked his arms around her just before her chairback landed hard on the wood floor. Sarah screamed, Onyx barked, and a cracking noise splintered the air as two bullets slugged into the cabinet right over where they'd been sitting.

TWO

Sarah cried out and rolled away from the upended chair. She crawled toward the pantry door as Onyx barked furiously beside them. Tucker followed, keeping the table between them and the window.

"Stay down." Tucker gripped a gun, his features taut with concentration. Onyx crouched beside them, his large triangular ears perked and a steady whine coming from his throat.

"Where are they, boy?" Tucker whispered to his dog. "Show me." He let go of the leash, and Onyx bear-crawled silently to the front door. When the door handle jangled, the dog let out a volley of barking that exploded through the kitchen. Sarah flinched.

Pounding footsteps sounded from the porch, then an engine roared nearby, followed by squealing tires.

"They're leaving." He scrambled to the window and peeked outside. Onyx panted beside him, eyes keen on the door. "A black minivan. Different vehicle." He watched it for several seconds before turning and padding back over to her. He kneeled so they were eye to eye.

"Did you see Liam?" Sarah choked on a sob.

"I'm sorry, I didn't. Are you hurt?"

She shook her head. "I'm okay." *No*, she wasn't. She was terrified for her son's life. It was cold and dark outside, and the two men who killed her husband now had her sweet seven-year-old. There must be a third person, the one shooting at them. Her heart turned to stone. It felt like she would never be okay again.

"I'm sorry I hit you so hard. We had to get down quickly. You sure you're okay?"

She tried to nod, but instead tears burned her eyes. Where was Liam?

In the distance, the wail of sirens sounded. *The police.*

"Listen. We are going to find him." His sympathetic gaze swept over her, cataloging her dirt and tear-streaked face. She'd always known Tucker was a compassionate person, and right now his concern was a safety net holding her together when it felt like she might otherwise shatter into a million pieces.

Please, God. I'll do anything. Please protect my son. Help the police find him.

"He must be so scared."

"If he's anything like his mom, he'll be strong and brave." A muscle in Tucker's jaw twitched as he withdrew his cell and answered a call. "Yeah, shots were fired, but Onyx warned us in time. He spooked them. Right. A black Dodge Caravan. Maybe five, six years old. Believe it was one suspect, just outside the front cottage door. I couldn't see the tags."

He listened for a few moments before saying *thanks* and ending the call.

"Two officers just arrived." He met her eyes. "One is searching for the shooter. They saw taillights when they pulled up. The other officer is Heath Calhoun. Do you remember him from that summer you were here?"

Her mind dialed back to those two months she trained in Erie, near Holloway. Her mom finally had landed a full-time job at a department store and couldn't leave Hagerstown, where Sarah had grown up and the two had shared an apartment. During the week, Sarah had lived at the dorms on-site at the Erie Aquatics Center, but on the weekends Aunt Beverly picked her up and brought her to the cottage. She met several young people in Holloway that summer, but she couldn't pull up any recognition of that name or a face to go with it.

"I'm sorry, I d-don't remember him right now."

"This has been a stressful day, and it was a long time ago." He rubbed a hand down his face. "Heath and I want to get you somewhere safe tonight while we're searching for Liam. Staying here isn't an option, I'm afraid."

She blinked up at the ceiling. All she could think about was the horrible man grabbing her son and throwing him into the car. "What if I leave the cottage and..." She searched for the right words, for a coherent thought.

"What if the men bring him back?" Tucker finished her question.

"Yes." Her throat tightened and the room blurred. "I want to be here if they...if he returns."

"The officers need time to check the cottage and the area around it for prints and possible clues." He shifted his gaze. "It's a crime scene."

She hiccupped on a sob.

He gently pressed an arm around her shoulders, comforting her with his strength and presence. "An officer will be stationed here for the next few hours. Then, if Liam makes it back, a friendly face will be here to keep him safe until you return. Would that make you feel better?"

She nodded, her emotions tipping toward tears again. "Yes. Thank you. I just want to find my son. I can't lose him too." A wave of shame crashed over her. "Tucker. I'm so sorry. I've been thinking only about myself. You just lost your brother.

I was busy worrying about my situation, about Liam, and I didn't consider your feelings."

"You are now." His eyes clung to hers. "I appreciate that, but right now I'm focused on finding Liam. Tanner and I..." His voice faded away for a moment. "We weren't exactly on speaking terms."

"But Tanner said he called you every couple of months."

Tucker shook his head, and she blinked furiously at the floor. The fact that Tanner was gone couldn't numb the painful realization that he had lied to her about yet another thing.

"Tuck." A broad-shouldered, brown-haired officer stepped into the house, his utility belt jangling. Onyx's tail wagged in greeting, immediately putting her at ease.

"Heath." Tucker shook his hand, then the officer turned to Sarah.

"Ma'am, I'm Sergeant Calhoun. Nice to see you back here, though I'm sorry it's under these circumstances." He grimaced.

"Thank you for coming out here so quickly. I can't believe all this happened. I shouldn't have run after I saw Tanner's murder. I should've stayed in Fountain View. It's just... I always felt safer here." She shuddered. "Now I'm not sure I'll ever feel safe again."

Sergeant Calhoun—Heath—held up a hand. "Holloway *is* a safe place, but unfortunately criminals are everywhere. My officers and I will do the very best we can to locate your son and find these guys. First, I'd like to get your official statement at the station. Second, here's where we're at. There's an APB out and three officers on duty tonight. Two are tracking the roads in and out of Holloway, and the third will go over the cottage and detail the crime scene here. One more thing." Heath cocked his head. "Mrs...?"

"It's Brindley." Her mouth felt dry and coarse like sandpaper. "It was Baxter when I was here years ago. Call me Sarah, please."

"That's right. So, Tucker mentioned a cat was kidnapped, too?"

"Yes." She rattled off a description of Mr. Meow.

"Got it. Say, you were the swimmer, right?" When she nodded, he continued. "Congratulations on those two medals. Tucker made us have a big ol' watch party the day you swam your event. He would've had a second one for that relay, but it was too short notice."

"A watch party?" She turned to find Tucker leaning down, scratching Onyx's ears.

"Sure," Heath answered. "It felt like we were cheering on a hometown hero in that pool."

"Thank you. It was an exciting day." She worked up an appreciative smile, then snuck another look at Tucker. He had straightened and now watched Heath with narrowed eyes.

Heath shrugged. "Anywho. Is your vehicle in the garage out back?"

"Yes." She'd driven her silver Mercedes SUV, the vehicle Tanner bought for her after the accident last year. She would've preferred her ten-year-old Chevy Tahoe, which smelled like chlorine and reminded her of the pool and when she'd brought home Liam as an infant, nestled in his car seat. But the accident had wrecked the passenger side, and it hadn't been salvageable.

"Tucker, how about you take Sarah to the station first? I'll be along after you. Shouldn't be more than ten, fifteen minutes. I want to follow up with my officer."

Tucker caught Sarah's attention. "You good with that?"

"Yes." She hated to leave the last spot where she'd been with Liam, but logically she knew she couldn't stay here.

Still, her chest caved in as she shuffled outside, the trampled bushes in front of the porch and the tire marks on the road evidence of the scuffle that had stolen the only thing that truly mattered to her, the only good thing she could offer this world.

Please, God. Bring Liam home.

Tucker turned on the engine and clicked up the heat as he and Sarah settled in his Bronco. It had been a mild winter so far, but colder weather and snow were forecasted to arrive soon. Just in time for Christmas. He released a sigh. It was difficult to even consider the holiday now that Liam was missing and Tanner was dead. His mom would be devastated.

Onyx whined from the back.

"He doesn't like being in the backseat. He'd rather be in the middle of the action. Or on my lap," he chuckled.

She reached back, stroking Onyx's neck. "What a handsome boy. Liam would love you. Mr. Meow, not so much." Her soft smile sank into a frown.

He turned the Bronco around and drove back the way he'd come an hour earlier, allowing her time to process her emotions in silence.

"Does Onyx work with you at the forest service?" she finally asked.

"Yes." He nixed the urge to tell her part of the reason why—that he'd been attacked by two cybercriminals attempting to destroy evidence last year at the ranger station. "His handler was in a fatal car accident, and Heath asked if I wanted a K9 partner at the district office. It's been a bit of a learning curve but well worth it."

"That's sad, but I'm glad you found each other. Do you still enjoy working as a forest ranger?"

"I can't imagine doing anything else. I'm the assistant supervisor of the Holloway District. Working under Mike Timmons." He flashed a brief smile. "Waiting for him to retire."

"It's the perfect job for you. I'll never forget how you rescued me on Bent Creek that day. Remember that big storm?"

"I do." Like he could ever forget the first time he saw her. "It was a doozy. A tornado spawned near the dam."

"The rain was so bad I couldn't see ten feet in front of me, and you just walked through it like some kind of guardian angel."

Her gratitude warmed him. "Not sure I rescued you. More like I was in the right place at the right time."

"You were there when I needed you. That's all that matters." She paused, and the interior of his car shrank at her sincere words. "Just like tonight."

His job as a forest ranger never felt like work. It was all he wanted to do—protect and care for God's creation. Help his community connect with the beautiful forest. And have a family. Be a loving dad like his father had in his short lifetime.

Tucker turned off Old Forge Road, gripping the steering wheel. When he glanced over at Sarah, tears tracked down her cheeks, and her stricken expression broke his heart. He reached over and settled his right hand on her arm.

"Hey, we *will* find him."

"I feel like I'm drowning, Tucker. Like I can barely breathe with him gone."

Maybe he could stir up some positive memories instead of this overwhelming pain she felt.

"What's Liam like? I sure wish I knew him better." He pulled his arm back.

She swiped at the tears. "He's so smart. I know I'm biased, but he really is. He gets computers and technology in ways I never did, and he can build a complicated LEGO set in an hour with no help from me. Liam also likes math best—math, of all subjects."

She paused, and when he looked over at her, Tucker was pleased to see a smile peeking out through her gloom.

"He's obsessed with your mom's—with Nanna's—chocolate chip cookies, and he loves Doritos. Oh, get this. Liam requests sliced apples and cheese cubes in his lunch every day."

"That's pretty healthy."

She nodded slowly, her smile slipping.

"What about sports? Swimming?"

"He did start swimming on the junior team this past summer."

"Like mother, like son."

"He prefers soccer," she admitted as Tucker slowed at a turn, using the opportunity to take in her lighter expression. "And he loves Mr. Meow. We got him because…"

"Because he wanted a cat?"

"More like he *needed* the cat." She hesitated. "Liam and I were in a car accident last year, and he had nightmares afterward. Also, Tanner and I have had a rough couple of years, and our relationship made Liam…upset. Worried. Things were often…rocky in our marriage."

"What do you mean, *rocky*?" From time to time since they'd married, Tucker let his thoughts wander to his twin and Sarah. He had wondered if Tanner truly appreciated Sarah or if his brother just saw her as an attractive woman—an Olympic-level athlete—who looked good on his arm. There was much more to her, so much depth, and Tucker had hoped his brother appreciated that.

It didn't sound like it.

She was silent for several heartbeats, staring out the passenger window. Had Tanner been physical with her or Liam? Tucker's blood pressure rose with every hard thump of his heart. He and Tanner had had plenty of scuffles during their younger years. But Tucker and Tanner had been equally matched—physically, at least. Sarah might be athletic and strong, whip fast in the pool, and a streak of lightning when she ran, but she was no match for Tanner.

"Sarah..." He gentled his voice even though he wanted to growl like Onyx. "Did Tanner hurt you or Liam?"

"No. Not physically." She ran her fingers along her jeans. "But we didn't have a peaceful marriage. I...frustrated him. And sometimes I couldn't keep my mouth shut about his work. He was already under a lot of stress, and it made him angry when I didn't outright support him in everything he did and said."

"I'm sorry to hear that." Memories inundated him from the summer they met. Sarah sharing about her alcoholic mom and the string of unruly boyfriends her mom brought home. How one of them had tried to hurt Sarah when she was fifteen, and how she'd jumped out of her second-story bedroom window, breaking her ankle in the process and missing out on a major swim meet. "What's going on with his job? Was he under threat of being fired or something?"

"Not exactly. But there's been a lot of pressure about that new medication."

"Strange that my mom never mentioned it." He spoke with their mom at least once a week, though now that he was thinking of it, his mom hadn't shared as many details about Tanner, Sarah or Liam the last couple months. "Tanner does visit her, right?"

"Once in a while." Her words were laced with frustration and something else. Regret? "I take Liam to see your mom a couple times each week. Since she can't drive, we usually go out and grab a bite to eat or walk at the park and feed the ducks, or I bring her over to spend the day."

"My mom can't drive?" He jerked his gaze to Sarah. "I had no idea her Parkinson's had gotten worse."

"I'm sorry to be the bearer of more bad news, but it has."

Tucker blinked dazedly into the night. A few years ago, Tanner told him he wanted their mom closer to him so that he could take care of her. Allow her to see her grandson frequently. *He's her only grandchild*, Tanner had ribbed him. Holloway was small and options were limited for senior activities, he had said.

A set of brights in the rearview mirror pierced the wintry darkness and Tucker's thoughts. His muscles tensed. They were ten minutes from Holloway proper, driving on Route 62. Heath said he would be a few more minutes so it was likely not him.

"What is it?" Sarah asked.

"Just making sure we're not being tailed."

She turned in her seat, and Onyx released a low whine and shook in his harness. One thing Tucker had learned quickly was how in tune with him the dog was. Almost like he could read Tucker's mind.

The headlights closed in on them steadily. "Just to be safe, will you lean down in your seat?"

She ducked low, her hair brushing his hand.

"That's good. Onyx, down."

They entered a construction zone. Parallel lines of orange cones marked where the two lanes merged into one and where the roadwork began. He merged to the other lane, and the vehicle tailing him did the same but remained about thirty yards back. Halfway through the construction zone, Tucker sped up, pushing the Bronco to twenty over the forty-mile-per-hour-speed limit. The other car accelerated as well, closing the gap.

He slipped his cell from his pocket and used his face to open it, then handed it to Sarah. "Hit 9-1-1, please."

She tapped the numbers on his phone, her hands shaking,

and he glanced down to see that the call was sending. Heath needed to know they had a tail.

Suddenly, the interior flooded with light.

"Hang on!" he shouted just as the other vehicle zoomed so close that it filled the rearview mirror. *The black van.*

The van smashed his bumper, pushing them forward. Sarah screamed and Onyx yelped, his harness holding him fast. Tucker's cell thudded to the floorboard as his Bronco recoiled from the impact. Orange cones flew into the air like a bowling ball crashing into pins as his front fender smashed into them. He forced the Bronco back in the lane, then accelerated until their surroundings were a dark blur. His four-wheel-drive SUV was made for off-road, for snow and ice traction on the Pennsylvania hills, not for speed.

He veered left as the van closed in on them again, clipping his bumper on the passenger side and throwing off the Bronco's momentum. Sarah gripped the console and the door with both hands, her breaths coming in gasps. He held his car steady, then edged away from the concrete wall, his mind whirling in a million directions like the cones he'd struck.

The minivan had to be a turbo engine, because he couldn't shake them. And if he didn't get away from it soon, one of their vehicles wouldn't survive this confrontation.

THREE

Sarah ducked beneath the dash, bracing herself with one hand and searching for Tucker's cell phone with the other. The call had gone through, but she hadn't had a chance to say anything before the car chasing them struck Tucker's bumper.

"They can tell where we are, right?" She had vague memories of driving through Holloway, but it had been years since she'd been here, so she had no idea if they were close to the police station.

"Yes. Sit up and hold on." Tucker let off the gas, and she straightened in her seat and gripped the door handle. Suddenly, he turned left, and she fought to keep from slamming into the passenger-side door. "Sorry, I'm trying to lose them."

"Where are we going?" Directly after the turn, they began climbing a steep paved road.

"This is Drussel Hill Road. It's a shortcut into Holloway that bisects a mountain."

No wonder it was so steep. Her back pressed into the seat as they ascended the sharply inclined road. She pushed off and turned. Headlights trailed behind, starting up the hill just a short distance back. "He's following."

"That's the plan." Tucker's gaze jumped from the rearview mirror to the narrow, winding street edged by thick woods.

She leaned down to search for the phone again. "You want

them to follow us?" Her fingers hit hard plastic. Tucker's phone. "Here's your cell."

"Good. Yes, I want them following us. We're going off road." Tucker turned right, steering them directly into a dark fold of trees. Gravel kicked up under the Bronco's tires. "They just cleared this land, and the road isn't paved yet. It's going to be bumpy."

Tucker's bright beams revealed a newly plowed road hedged in by cut-down trees stacked haphazardly along the roadside. From what she could make out in the dark, iced-over mud puddles and rocks dotted the impassable stretch of crushed woods. She gritted her teeth as he adeptly maneuvered his vehicle, her head wobbling with each pothole. When they came to the end, she turned. The minivan's headlights were barely visible behind them. They'd fallen back. Or gotten stuck.

She squinted. "Do you think they have Liam?"

"Doubt it. They had him in the Camry. Do me a favor, please? Call 9-1-1 again?"

She hit 9-1-1, then the speaker button, and Tucker spoke to the dispatcher. "There's a black minivan in Sunrise Valley, off Drussel Hill. I believe it's the vehicle that fired shots at Beverly Baxter's cottage on Old Forge Road thirty minutes ago. It appears to be stuck. I need officers up here ASAP."

He got confirmation, hung up the cell and then accelerated his Bronco. A glowing yellow streetlight shone ahead. "There we go. We'll be back on Drussel Hill Road, which connects to Holloway Valley Road in town." Tucker's confidence doused her fired-up nerves. "We'll be at the police station in five minutes at this rate."

Soon they descended the mountain, then spilled out onto Holloway Valley Road. Her mind clouded with the image of the man who'd attacked her. If only Liam hadn't come outside. He must've heard her screams and been trying to help her. *Oh, my brave Liam.*

She kneaded her fingertips into her brows and closed her eyes.

Please, God, keep him safe. Please bring him back to me.

Prayer had never been a comfortable conversation for her. Oh, she'd tried praying from time to time when life became too much to handle on her own, but she had no idea how to actually do it. Mainly because the idea of God as a loving father in Heaven never sat well with her. She'd had so few good examples of caring, faithful men in her life. Still, for her son's sake, she had to try. Had to believe God cared about Liam despite what she had done in her life.

"Hey, he's going to be okay." Tucker's voice found her lost and brought her back to herself. "This may be a small town, but we have technology just like Fountain View and capable law enforcement in this area."

"Thank you." *Please, God. Let it be true.*

"The first thing I want to do is build a LEGO set with him."

"I would love that. For both of you." Her heart seized as she pictured Tucker beside Liam, poring over a LEGO set. Patient as ever. "Tanner...rarely had time."

Tucker parked in front of the police station, staring straight ahead for several seconds. Then he turned the ignition off and looked her way, sadness and something else etched on his features. Regret?

Suddenly, his hand engulfed hers, warming her clear through. "We're going to get him back, Sarah, and I'll make time. I promise."

She nodded once, clinging to the determination and compassion she saw in his eyes. Right now, it was her lifeline.

Tucker guided Sarah to one of the chairs facing Heath's desk in his office, then he sank into the other one. Onyx padded in a circle twice then lay down, resting his muzzle on his front paws.

He had taken a quick look at his bumper before they came inside. The Bronco had sustained a solid hit, but the damage was minimal—a small dent and a two-inch scratch—thanks to the higher carriage of his SUV from the XL tires. Sarah had apologized profusely, but he'd waved it off.

"It's a thing. You're a person. Your life is infinitely more valuable than my car."

Sarah had gaped at him as though she'd never heard such a statement, and Tucker's heart had taken a dive. Had his brother ever made her feel loved and valued? Had Tanner ever told Sarah that she was kind, strong and caring?

Sitting in the quiet police station at ten o'clock at night, Tucker settled his weary gaze on Heath. Tucker had just gotten off a brief call with his supervisor, Ranger Mike Timmons. Mike had posted the kidnapping and the details about Liam's appearance and clothing on the US Forest Service website, which triggered a text to each of the rangers in Allegheny National Forest and the surrounding areas within a one-hundred-mile radius.

Tucker reached over and stroked Onyx's head. He needed to call his mom and break the news about Tanner and Liam, but he'd do that tomorrow morning. Talk about heartbreaking.

Lord, I always need Your help, but now I really need it. Sarah and Liam do too.

Heath tossed his cell on the desk with a resounding *thud*, then reached back to rub his neck. He scrutinized Tucker before addressing Sarah.

"I realize I didn't say this at the cottage. I want to offer my sympathies on the loss of your husband. I didn't know Tanner as well as I do Tucker, but it's a tragic and senseless loss, and I'm very sorry."

She clasped her hands as though in prayer. "Thank you."

"I also want to let you know all my officers are on the lookout for the Camry and your son. The Pennsylvania Highway Patrol know about the situation as well. At this very moment we're checking out the minivan on Drussel Hill too. Tucker?"

Tucker leaned forward and rested his elbows on his knees. "I notified Mike, my supervisor, and he put an alert out to the rangers here and across the state. We have all hands on deck, Sarah."

She turned, her grateful gaze roving his face and making him feel like he could take on the world. Then she looked back at Heath. "I'm grateful for all your help."

"Now, about the case," Heath continued, and Tucker returned his attention to his friend. "At this point, even without a ransom note, I'm fairly confident your son's kidnapping is tied to Tanner's murder. So, I need to know exactly what occurred at your husband's office earlier today."

Sarah exhaled sharply, then recounted the events with Heath as she had with Tucker in the cottage. Near the end, she glanced between the men. "Tanner oversees one of the production lines at Zeta Pharmaceuticals. Their latest drug targets advanced Parkinson's patients. It had just come through clinical trials. But a problem occurred during the trials." She ran her fingers down her chin. "Something that caused issues between Tucker and his coworkers on the project. There were lengthy conversations and…arguments."

"Did you hear any of the conversations? Or the arguments?" Heath asked.

"Bits and pieces. It was hard to make sense of it, and Tanner kept things at work pretty private."

"Those companies are highly competitive," Tucker noted. "They don't want their new formulas or medicines or whatnot getting into competitors' hands."

"Right." Heath jotted down a note. "So, were there any arguments *you* had with him that might pertain to this investigation? And why were you at his work today?"

"The other day he was working on the clinical trial reports, and I happened to go down the hall near our office downstairs. I'd been getting Liam ready for bed upstairs, and I don't think he heard me walk by the office. When I caught what he said…"

She glanced at Tucker, her smooth brow wrinkled and an apology in her eyes.

"Sarah, what did you hear?" he prompted gently.

"Tanner was talking about your mom. He said your mom—Sharlene—had been part of the initial clinical trial pool, and the outcome wasn't what he wanted. Some…side effects had occurred that made him question the product's safety. And she wasn't the only one who had problems."

Tucker stood, his chair scooting back at the abrupt motion. Onyx lifted his head and whined, then stood too. "He used our mom in one of the clinical studies?"

Sarah held her palm out. "Please don't be mad at me. But yes, he did."

"I'm not mad at you. Don't think that for a second. I'm furious at my brother."

She continued, and he forced himself to listen to her words and not the hive of bees buzzing in his brain. "One of the reasons I was going into his work this morning was to question him about Sharlene and demand he take her out of the trials."

"He never asked me for permission." Tucker's pulse kicked up a couple of notches as he paced. "Did *she* approve of being part of this clinical trial? Wait a minute—is that why her health tanked?"

"I'm not sure. But that's what I wondered, and that's one of the reasons I was going to confront him out of our house, where Liam wouldn't be subject to it." Her gaze fell to her lap. "That, and other things."

He was all for medication when it was necessary and needed. It saved lives, sure. But to use their mom for the clinical trials, without asking Tucker's position or thoughts?

Heath's cell beeped. He grabbed it, hit the speaker button. "Calhoun here. What's up?"

"Hey, Sarge. We found the black minivan on Drussel Hill Road. Front tire is stuck in a pothole, and the vehicle is abandoned."

Tucker sat back in the chair, and Onyx sank to his haunches. The driver had run off. Sarah leaned forward, listening.

"We notified the residents within a two-mile radius. There's only a few," the officer continued. "No sign of the driver or of the boy. We're checking for prints inside the vehicle and footprints around it."

Tucker pinched the bridge of his nose. The suspects must've kept Liam in the Camry. Where had they taken him?

His thoughts circled around to what Sarah just shared. Tanner must've moved their mom closer to him so he could include her in the clinical trial—something Tucker would've balked at had he known his brother's intention. At the very least, Tucker would've wanted more information. Had Tanner been trying to pull the drug because their mom had had negative reactions to the medication?

He was aware of the astronomical profits from the pharmaceutical industry. While in pharmaceutical sales, Tanner's salary undoubtably had been quadruple what Tucker's forest ranger salary was. Now, as the head of the product-creation team, Tanner could've been pulling in half a million a year, easy. Drugs were big business, and a promising new medication on the horizon would gain wide and powerful interest in pharmaceutical and medical circles.

Was the threat of losing out on millions of dollars reason enough to kill his brother—and come after Sarah?

FOUR

Sarah climbed into Tucker's Bronco and buckled her seat belt while he situated Onyx in the back. He opened the driver's-side door and folded inside, his movements slow and methodical. He must be as exhausted as she was.

She'd finished giving her statement, and they were headed to Tucker's house for the night. Relief spilled through her that she wouldn't be alone.

While she appreciated Heath's confidence and Tucker's presence, she missed her son. Missed his voice and his laugh and his funny comments. Every moment since he was taken felt like a battle against tears. Against collapsing into a broken heap.

Against a deluge of questions there were no answers for.

"Hey," he murmured. "We're going to find him."

She nodded once—all she could offer without breaking down—then gazed out the window as they exited the police station. Nighttime enveloped Allegheny National Forest in a pitch-dark cloak made all the heavier by the bleakness of winter.

It was after 11:00 p.m., and her body ached with a weariness that made her limbs listless. She must've bruised her tailbone when the attacker threw her off the porch or when the car sent her flying.

"If you're hungry, I have leftover pizza and wings in the fridge."

She rolled her head against the headrest. "Thank you, but I don't think I can eat tonight." She wasn't sure she could eat until Liam was back in her arms.

Tucker guided the car through the dimly lit roads in Holloway. Every now and then, a pair of brights would break through the dark, and his hands would strangle the steering wheel until the car passed by. His mannerisms were so different from Tanner's—how he'd listened intently, head tilted, while she relayed what happened at the cottage, the way his intense gaze followed her as she spoke, even his stride. Steady and cautious, not vigorous and purposeful like Tanner's.

Tucker had always fascinated her. He was strong but not threatening. Quiet but surprisingly funny. Handsome but not arrogant. And he had never made her feel uncomfortable like most adult males, even Tanner, who had basically been in the driver's seat of their relationship from day one. As a twenty-year-old with little dating history and a healthy aversion to men, she had found Tanner's interest intimidating at first, but eventually she'd been caught up in the force of his attention. Once she knew he wouldn't hurt her the way her mom's boyfriend had tried to, she'd been all in.

Too bad she hadn't recognized Tanner's inherent selfishness. How focused on appearances and others' thoughts he was underneath his confident veneer.

Tucker reminded her more of their thoughtful, caring mom than Tanner ever had.

"Poor Sharlene. Should we call her?" She glanced his way, the dim light from the highway's streetlights revealing his grim expression.

"She's been asleep for three hours. I don't want to wake

her with this news. It's a double whammy. Tanner's death and Liam's kidnapping."

The reminder about her missing son made her flinch. "Maybe you should drive down to Fountain View tomorrow to tell her."

"No. I'm not leaving you until we find Liam." His decisive words brooked no argument. "I think I'll call Aunt Nell. My mom's younger sister?"

"Good idea. She's been so helpful with your mom's doctors visits this fall. With my coaching schedule and Liam's school, sometimes I can't take her."

"I'll see if Nell can swing by, and that way she'll be with Mom when I break the news."

The road narrowed to two lanes as they drove out of Holloway, and the highway lights faded, leaving them in a black tunnel that raised chill bumps on her limbs. She rubbed them, and Tucker clicked up the heat.

A boulder settled on her chest. "Usually, I like winter—Christmas and all—but at the moment I can't handle the cold or think about the holidays."

"You've been under intense stress the last twenty-four hours. Your body is struggling to keep up."

"Definitely feels that way." She peered through the windshield. "Do you live near the forest service station?"

"Pretty close. It's about an eight-minute drive from my place."

Five minutes later they entered a long, narrow lane that opened to a wide field. A barn with another structure jutting off it—like a renovated barn-turned-house—was situated on the right side of the field. An oversize two-door garage attached by a breezeway sat on the barn's other side, and a pond glittered opposite the house. The setting struck a familiar chord and made her feel lighter.

"Wait. Isn't this the place your youth group took us for movies the summer I was here? Didn't they own a bunch of goats?" The barn's back side had been used to project movies at one time, and a large pasture filled most of the far field, complete with a pond and small fishing dock.

"Who can forget the goats?" He grinned as he put his Bronco in park. "You're right. I bought this property from the Howards last year."

"That's it. Howards' Family Farm." She had accompanied Tanner and Tucker when they chaperoned their former youth group one Saturday night. They'd petted and fed goats and chased chickens. The owners had provided s'mores and a kitchen table–size bonfire over which to cook them. Afterward, they'd watched a popular cartoon movie about zoo animals on the back of the barn.

Sarah chuckled. "You saved my marshmallow that night."

"Say what?"

"I was trying to make the perfect marshmallow, and right before I finished, it fell into the logs. You used a free roasting stick, speared it and gave it to me." She licked her lips. "It was just a little burned on one side, kind of crunchy, but otherwise perfect." Their gazes connected in the car, and her mouth dried out at the look of longing in his eyes.

"So, you like crunchy marshmallows, do you?"

She scrunched up her nose in a quick grin. "I did that night."

Onyx whined, breaking apart the electric connection of memory and something more.

"That was a long time ago." His throat bobbed on a swallow, then he reached across her to open the glove compartment, extracting a flashlight and firearm. They climbed out at the same time, the previous moment's intensity dissipating as he released Onyx. The dog bounded out, and Tucker retrieved a black backpack from the seat.

The biting winter air, mixed with the earthy smells of the forest, filled her nose, and stars peeked through swaths of racing clouds. In the distance, the wind whistled through the trees, and the jangle of Onyx's leash and collar tinkled like sleigh bells. If she had Liam, and Tanner hadn't just been murdered, this would feel like a moment to savor.

"He can run loose out here?"

"Oh yeah. No one lives within a couple miles. He won't go far." Tucker unclicked the K9's collar from the leash. "Check it out." He pushed out his hand, palm up, and Onyx stopped, sniffed the bushes and ground, then beelined for the back of the barn-turned-house.

"How'd you manage to buy this?"

"It helped that I saved the Howards' dog from a poacher's trap," he answered matter-of-factly. "Boomer went too far one day on a run and never came home. The Howards asked for my help, and I tracked him to a spot in the forest near the open hunting lands. He had been chasing a couple deer and ended up in the wrong spot."

"Poor thing. Was he okay?"

"Walks with a bit of a limp now, but at least the vet saved his leg. Between the termite infestation in their house, their advancing age and wanting to be closer to family in Charleston, I finally convinced them to sell. Told them I'd take care of the place and keep it up. Other than tearing the old house down and turning the barn into a residence."

"It looks like you just painted it?" As she admired the large structure, her eyes caught on a tree stump edging the front door, an eagle carved into the wood.

"Yep. This summer. It's a five-year project. Maybe ten." He chuckled, and the sound made her smile. "It's livable inside, but don't expect a four-star hotel."

"I'm sure it's fine. Aunt Bev's cottage smelled like mothballs and sour milk. Liam even noticed it." She gulped at the memory of his quip about the scent of the older cottage.

Tucker set his hand lightly on the small of her back. "Let's get inside."

Warmth spread through her at the contact. As they treaded toward the breezeway connecting the two-door garage and the barn, Onyx appeared around the corner of the building, his tongue rolling out and eyes bright. The dog trotted over to Tucker then sat.

"Good boy." Tucker scratched his ears. "I know what you want." He reached around to his backpack and pulled out a stuffed animal so mangled it was nearly unidentifiable. A giraffe, maybe. "This is Jerry. Well, *was* Jerry."

Sarah smiled as Tucker tossed the giraffe to Onyx, who snatched it in his powerful jaws and shook the animal several times. He trotted around, head high and tail out like a flag.

Tucker stepped ahead of her, striding toward the breezeway. It was then that she noticed more of the stumps, lined up beside the barn. A dozen or so, different shapes and types of tree trunks. Another eagle, this one with spread wings; a mother deer and fawn; a chunky bear sitting on its backside eating berries; small intricately carved scenes with squirrels; and one that even appeared to be a fox with two kits.

"Didn't you use to carve things in wood?" When she turned to him, he avoided meeting her eyes. "Wait. Tucker, are those yours?"

His gaze lingered on the tree stumps for several heartbeats, then he stepped up to the door and tapped in a code. "You remember I liked to carve?"

"Yes, I remember. They're amazing, so intricately detailed." The lock beeped and flashed green, and they entered a shadowed hallway. "You could easily sell those."

"It's mostly just a hobby." He shrugged. "Maybe one day."

Then he motioned her forward, Onyx following. Tucker locked the door and trailed after her as she moved deeper into the high-ceilinged structure.

A click near her ear turned on an overhead lamp, and she squinted at the bright light in what appeared to be the kitchen area. The faint scent of cedar and cinnamon added a homey sensation to the half-finished cabinets.

"Sorry about that. I'll dim it. I have most of my lights and the cameras outside on motion sensors—some on timers too. Here." He tapped something on his phone screen, and the light dimmed.

"Through here is the main area of the house. It's part of the original barn, as you can see, and that's where the bedrooms are." He pointed. "If you don't mind, I prefer you sleep in my room, in the loft. There's a queen-sized bed and a futon that turns into a comfortable bed too. Only thing is, there's no door. Is that okay?"

"Yes, thank you. It's just..." She sighed as the boulder rolled back over her chest. "I don't think I can sleep with Liam gone."

"Understandable. But I think you should still try. We have a lot of officers on duty tonight looking for him, and we need you to rest and be strong for when we get him back."

She set her lips tightly together and nodded, feeling like a wilting flower. Like she'd never be strong again.

"I'll stay downstairs." He pointed to the center of the large open room, where an L-shaped sectional faced a nearby wall. A large-screen TV took up part of the wall, and a shelving unit holding a bunch of books and smaller wood carvings sat beside it. Situated on a small coffee table, a two-foot-high Christmas tree sparkled. There were four sets of windows in the barn section of the house and one long window that stretched from the first floor up to the second—the loft he'd mentioned, which faced the attached garage.

Two skylights opened up on the roof, long rectangular slices of cloudy winter night.

He pulled out his cell phone. "If you don't mind, I need to call my aunt."

She winced, sending him a compassionate look. "Take your time." She wandered into the living room area, stroking the Christmas tree's soft needles as he headed back into the kitchen, his voice rising and falling in conversation.

Five minutes later, Tucker approached the couch, where she sat flipping through a dog-eared wood-working magazine.

"How is she?" Sarah gently asked.

"Shocked. Upset. Aunt Nell never had kids, you know, and Tanner and I were like surrogate sons. I promised I'd call tomorrow and see how things are once she arrives at Mom's." He rubbed a palm down his face. "We'll all have to work together on the funeral arrangements."

Funeral arrangements. The finality of those words put her lungs in a vise grip. *Please, God, only for Tanner. Not for Liam too.*

She rose on shaky legs. "Listen, about tonight. I can sleep on the sofa."

"I prefer you stay upstairs. I'll be down here. There's no way into the loft except through the first floor. Given what happened tonight, I think that's safest."

His steely voice and set jaw stopped her next words, and a chill chased down her spine.

Did he think the men could find her here too?

Tucker started up the spiral staircase after Sarah.

"You'll be fine, boy," he called down to Onyx. The tight, twisting metal stairs had proven to be Onyx's nemesis, and his faithful partner waited at the bottom with a disgruntled snort.

Most nights, Onyx chose to sleep on his dog bed downstairs beside the door, ever vigilant.

"There's a half bath up here," he said when they reached the top and entered the open loft. "Would you like water or anything to drink?"

She nodded her thanks, then he spun down the staircase and trod back into the kitchen. Onyx cavorted around him, pleased at his quick return. Sarah's presence at his place was the last scenario he'd ever expected. After all, his days of pining after his brother's girlfriend-turned-wife were long past, though Tucker couldn't deny the pull she still had on him. She was kind and smart, and he could spend hours—no, days—memorizing the nuances of her face and eyes. There was no denying the other women he'd dated through the years had been measured against her and, sadly, found lacking.

Don't even think it, Brindley. He withdrew a bottled water from the fridge, then grabbed a washcloth and hand towel from the downstairs closet and wound back up the stairs. Sarah sat cross-legged on the futon couch, leaning back on the cushion, eyes closed. Maybe she was already asleep.

Then her eyes opened, and worry replaced the momentary reprieve from the stressful day she wore on her face. He crossed the room, handed her the water and then set the towels on the bathroom sink. "Here's a washcloth and hand towel if you need them."

"Thank you." She took a long swig of the water. "I was just thinking about what happened today, at Tanner's work. Trying to go over the details, see if there's something I missed." Her voice faded to a whisper. "I can't believe he's…"

"I know. Me either."

"It still doesn't feel real." The water bottle crinkled in her grasp.

Tucker sat on the far edge of the futon mattress, making

sure his good ear faced her. "He drove me crazy at times, but he was my only brother. Only sibling. I wish..." His throat thickened as reality took a turn punching his gut. "I wish I could still talk to him. Make amends."

"I'm so sorry." She slid closer. "He rarely said it, but I could tell he respected you. Admired you."

"Yeah?" A half-smile worked on his mouth. "When we were young and cocky, Tanner and I used to take bets on who would own this place first."

"I don't think *you* were ever cocky. Why did you want the Howards' place?"

"Lots of reasons. I wanted to live near the forest. Have my own land. Stocked fishing pond? Pasture and barn? Yes, please. Maybe get some horses, a couple goats." He drew in a measured breath as dreams far out of reach drifted before his mind's eye.

"What about a family?"

"That too. One day." He hoped his voice wasn't as wistful as his thoughts. "This place represented some great times from my youth, and I didn't want some developer to get to it. I wanted more generations of young people to enjoy it here like we did." He frowned. Too bad his mouth didn't have a rewind button. No need to share all that with her.

"I'm glad you bought it. Tanner wouldn't have appreciated it like you do. Plus, he had enough in his life."

Like you, Tucker thought immediately.

He crossed his arms and glared at the ceiling. *Stop it. She could've chosen you, but she didn't. Tanner said she didn't want a boyfriend with hearing problems. End of story.*

"He never wanted to stay in Holloway," she admitted.

"Nope. Tanner had his sights set on bigger and better things. On a higher salary than he could ever make here."

"Money isn't everything," she noted quietly. "I think it

was his pursuit of money and prestige at Zeta that was his downfall."

He let her words settle before asking a question that had been on his mind, but he'd forgotten to inquire about earlier. "Tell me more about the disagreements Tanner had with his coworkers? Any issues with others or his boss?"

She rubbed her temples. "He and Mark Sousa butted heads."

"Who's this?"

"I guess I forgot to mention him. Mark Sousa is the pharmaceutical scientist Tanner worked with closely on the Parkinson's medication. He and his team designed and created the drug, then tested its effectiveness. Tanner was the liaison between upper management and Mark and his production team."

"The monkey in the middle," Tucker mused.

"Yes, you could say that."

"I assume Mark wanted the drug to pass clinical trials so it could get on the market ASAP."

"Of course," Sarah answered.

"And what about earlier today. Did you see Mark when you walked into Tanner's work this morning?"

"No. Although Mark works in the basement." She snorted. "It's not really a basement. It's a fancy laboratory with a bunch of security downstairs."

"Did the two of them get along?"

She pursed her lips. "Not really. Mark was pompous. Demanding. No, Tanner never liked seeing Mark's name on his caller ID."

His phone. Tucker straightened. "Do you know where Tanner's phone is?"

"I have it." Her eyes widened. "I went in to talk to him today about your mom, but I also had his cell. He'd left it on the kitchen counter. After Liam was taken, I forgot about that. I should've mentioned that to Heath."

"Is it here, with you?" He glanced at her purse on the nightstand.

"No, it's in my car at the cottage. I threw it in my bag when I packed to come to Holloway."

Tucker pulled out his cell and sent off a text to Heath. They'd need to secure Tanner's phone as soon as possible.

"What is it?" she straightened.

"The men coming after you may have been looking for that. There could be incriminating evidence on his cell. This is all speculation, of course. But it seems logical."

She yawned, and Tucker rose to his feet.

"I'll let you get some rest. Onyx and I will be keeping an eye and ear out."

"Good night, Tucker. Thank you for being there tonight."

"Anytime. Good night."

He headed downstairs, his chest hollowed out. Onyx met him at the last step, circling Tucker, his tail thumping. Then the dog looked over at the kitchen, where his leash hung. He wanted a run tonight, but that wasn't happening. Not now.

Not with Sarah here.

"Sorry, boy. Just a quick trip out then back inside. You're on guard duty with me tonight."

Onyx yipped, then sat, awaiting further instructions. Tucker checked the time before he strode through to the breezeway, his mind on Sarah, thoughts about what she'd shared churning. Tanner's cell phone. Could that be the key to figuring out who was after her and why they'd taken Liam?

As he reached for the door knob a light burst on across the property. He stopped and scanned the yard through the door sidelight. The old shed near the fishing pond. Onyx let out a ferocious growl that prickled the hairs on Tucker's neck. Had deer set it off?

He had been training Onyx to ignore deer. They ran through

his property almost daily. Could be a fox or a pack of coyotes, but normally Onyx didn't respond to animal intruders. Only *human* ones.

He scrambled toward the living room window, whistling softly for Onyx to follow.

"Tucker!"

Sarah's cry bounced through the barn's rafters, half shout, half scream, whipping him around. He faced the loft, weapon drawn. They'd been followed.

FIVE

Sarah slapped a hand over her mouth, every muscle quaking. Bright orange flames reflected off the loft's two-story window. She shouted Tucker's name again as the small fire climbed one corner of the attached garage on the other side of the breezeway.

Footsteps smacked the spiral staircase, and seconds later Tucker hustled over.

"What is—Is that a fire?" He gaped at the window then hauled her away from the glass.

A *whomp, ping* sound shattered the moment, and she gasped as the window she'd just been standing in front of fragmented into hundreds of pieces.

"Get down!" Tucker tugged her to the floor.

They hit the carpet together, and he caught her in his arms as they rolled toward the futon and far wall. From the first floor, Onyx barked several times.

"Stay!" he shouted at the dog.

Her entire body shook. "There's a fire in your garage."

"I saw that. I'm calling 9-1-1, then going outside to try and put out the fire. Listen, there's a crawl space downstairs. It leads to a cellar. Before Onyx and I go outside, I want you inside that."

While she was in the middle of processing his words,

Tucker lifted her upright, hurrying her down the stairs and through the living room. Halfway there he tapped the face of his phone. He was careful to keep them away from the windows as he urged her toward the far wall. A dispatcher's voice came on the line.

"Shots fired at my residence," Tucker informed the dispatcher. "I need to secure my property and get that fire out." He paused as the dispatcher spoke. "Yes. Tell Heath I'll be outside. Hurry!"

He ended the call, then leaned over and pushed a long engraved wooden chest away from the wall. She gaped as an opening came into view on the revealed wall, a few feet long and maybe two feet high, with a small, notched handle on one end. The crawl space.

Her pulse thrummed in her temples. "What if the fire catches on the house?"

"It won't. It's the far corner of the garage. But…" He paused. "If I don't return in five minutes, you can move deeper in and then slide down into a small cellar. It's a four-foot drop, so be careful. They used to use it to store canned items, and I never closed it up when I remodeled the floors. You'll see a small half door. It opens in the yard beside the barn."

He reached for the notched handle. After twisting it and tugging hard for a couple of seconds, the door made a sighing noise and released, sliding, then opening to a dark storage space that looked an awful lot like a mouth in the wall.

She shivered. "I hate tight spaces."

His features curved down in apology. "I can't leave you unprotected. If I go out there, and somehow one of them gets in here before authorities arrive…" He let his words drop off and glanced at his K9 partner. "Officers and a fire truck are on their way, but for now this is the safest spot. Please. When we find Liam, he'll need his mom."

The stubborn compassion in his gaze was her undoing. She kneeled, then half rolled, half crawled into the low spot. Something skinny and hard clacked against her feet.

"Those are my hunting rifles. They're not loaded."

"Right. I just have to worry about burning alive alone in here."

"You're not going to die. I'll make sure of that. God has much more in store for your life."

She stared up at him, hoping he saw the gratitude in her eyes. "Be safe out there." Then she wiggled all the way inside, stifling a moan at the closed-in feeling. He drew the door down, and her world turned dark.

God, please protect him, and please put out that fire.

Tucker pulled up the app on his phone that controlled his security system and all the lights inside and outside the barn, along with the shed. He tapped the off button, sending the area into pitch darkness. He knew this property better than anyone else, and he could use that to his advantage.

Plus, he had an extra set of eyes and ears in Onyx.

He replaced his cell in his pocket, then drew his Glock from his waistband, holding the weapon steady as he slunk across the living room. The barn's sturdier structure meant the walls were reinforced and the layout was unique—the criminals outside wouldn't know the floor plan or which door he would use to exit.

But the fire. He had to save his garage if he could. Save his woodworking tools and the unfinished projects inside. Keep it from breaching the breezeway. At least he hadn't parked his Bronco in there. Only his mom's twenty-year-old Civic still sat inside.

He sidled toward the barn's side door, opposite the breezeway. Thoughts of Sarah accompanied every stride.

Lord, help me and Onyx find these men, please. Keep us all safe.

He reached for the door handle, then pushed it open just wide enough to slip through. Onyx followed. The scent of smoke tainted the cold air, and adrenaline poured through his limbs as bursts of howling wind teased the flames higher. He slinked around the barn's back side, keeping his spine against the structure while facing the woods. Onyx shadowed him, and when the dog whined, Tucker slowed. As they closed in on the breezeway, Onyx's lithe body became agitated.

Tucker motioned for Onyx to stay, then he inched toward the corner that would lead them to the open breezeway. Suddenly, a dark form moved stealthily around the corner, just as Tucker had been. Tucker lunged at him, wrapping one arm around the man's neck. The suspect struggled and shouted, slamming his foot onto the tip of Tucker's boots, but Tucker tightened his chokehold. He didn't have handcuffs on him, and he couldn't risk the suspect running or making any more noise in case he had a partner. Once the man went limp, Tucker reached up and cracked the butt of his gun to his temple, sending him to the ground.

"Hold him," he told Onyx. "Stay." His partner's muzzle bumped the man's shoulder, his eyes laser focused on his captive. Tucker checked him for weapons. He retrieved a small gun and two knives and shoved them in his back pockets.

Tucker found his garden hose, wound up at the back of the garage. He took one more quick look around the area. Onyx was a capable, well-trained K9, but Tucker didn't want to risk leaving the suspect and dog alone too long.

Lord, help me get this fire out.

The wind picked up, howling. Shrouded in darkness, lit by the light of a hundred flames, the crackling pop of the wood being eaten alive by the fire pumped his pulse into overdrive.

He turned the spigot on, adjusted the spray nozzle and let the water loose. The stream shot out from the hose nozzle, spraying directly at the fire. He yanked more of the hose loose and circled the back of the garage to hit the base of the corner.

A sizzling pop sent him to his knees, and a prickle of pain needled his arm. His gaze swerved every which way. *The window.* Thermal stress from the heat had shattered the windowpanes, and pieces lay around the grass like glittering diamonds.

He glanced at his arm, where a trickle of blood streaked down to his fingers. Glass.

He continued spraying the fire, fighting as another gust of wind whipped across the field. Ice-cold water droplets skittered over his forehead and nose. Rain? His throat thickened.

Thank You, God.

The steady rain continued, soaking the garage roof and the barn and himself. Onyx's alerting bark, followed by movement to his left, snatched his focus from the dwindling fire to his house. A dark figure dashed through the shadowed yard from the nearest tree line straight for the barn's back doors.

Sarah.

"Onyx, go!"

The dog left his post beside the first suspect and sprinted toward the second man, who had disappeared around the building. Tucker dropped the hose and followed his partner toward the barn's back door. A cacophony of canine snarling and pained, human cries eclipsed the snapping, whipping flames. Onyx had made contact with the second suspect.

He adjusted his hold on his weapon as he jogged over. The man's arm was clamped between Onyx's jaws, and he shouted in pain, thrashing on the damp ground. Raindrops glittered in Onyx's coat, and the dog's ferocious growling filled the air as Tucker approached, his gun trained on the man.

"Get him off me!"

"Release!" Tucker shouted. "Put your hands in the air."

Onyx let the man go. In an instant, the suspect was on his feet and racing away from the barn's back doors, into the night. Onyx started to follow.

"Stay!" A dark pack lay on the ground near the door, and Onyx paced back and forth beside it then sat, panting heavily, his sharp eyes focused on Tucker as he waited for the next command.

His muscles turned to ice. Had the suspect left the pack on purpose?

A bomb. The second man had been attempting to place the pack in his house.

"Onyx, heel!" Tucker pivoted and sprinted away from the pack, Onyx at his side in two strides. A few heartbeats later an ear-splitting *boom* ricocheted across the grass, followed by a blast of heat that prickled his skin, then threw them forward with the energy of the explosion. An image of Sarah's face filled his mind before he slammed into the earth.

Sarah cried out as a massive *boom* shook the crawl space. Dust particles rained down on her, and she coughed as grit clouded the oxygen.

Her mouth dried out and her tongue turned to cotton. Maybe the fire had reached something flammable in Tucker's garage and set off an explosion.

Please, God, keep Tucker safe. Please bring Liam back to me.

She prayed he was warm, that he and Mr. Meow were together. Prayed that the fire would stop on Tucker's house. Prayed until the silence became oppressive.

How strange it was, praying fervently, when for many years she'd struggled to draw close to God. Shortly after she'd tried praying about her and Tanner's failing marriage, she'd discovered his infidelity. All the anger and hurt that had been roused in her she'd pushed toward God.

How could He let her go through this?

But one thing she never doubted was that Liam was a gift from God, her special blessing, and she would never stop thanking Him for her son despite the mess of her life.

"Sarah Brindley? You in here?"

She didn't recognize the voice. Goose bumps pebbled her limbs, and she curled her hands in, nails scoring her palms.

"Sarah?" A second voice joined the first, this one muffled but familiar. *Heath Calhoun.*

From inside her barricaded position, the faint peal of sirens carried through the wood. The fire department. She shoved at the crawl space with her hands and kicked with her feet, pounding and pushing from the inside. With a suction noise, it released and opened. She inhaled the clean air as she fell out of the opening.

A pair of dark brown men's work boots and the bottom of a uniform stopped in her line of sight. "Sarah?"

Suddenly she was pulled to her feet. Heath held her upright as her cramped muscles spasmed and stretched.

"Where's Tucker? And Onyx? Are they okay?"

"They're with the paramedics. Far as I can tell, your four-footed and two-legged heroes will be a-okay."

"I need to see them." She brushed past him on unsteady legs.

"Hey, slow down." Heath caught up to her. "Tucker is under medical supervision. No need to hurt yourself getting out there."

"What about Onyx?"

"Paramedics don't normally work on canines, but we'll take the dog up to Doc Schaffer to make sure he's okay too."

His words didn't exactly comfort her. There must be a reason the K9 would have to go to the vet. She inched around him and hurried for the back door, then let out a cry.

The door and its frame were gone, leaving a gaping hole in the back of Tucker's home. She turned, mouth slack, toward Heath. "Is this from the fire?"

"No, this is from a bomb. You may want to go around to—"

She ignored him as she climbed over the scorched wood pieces and chunks of charred concrete. The flashing red and white ambulance lights lit up the night, and she jogged across the damp grass to the emergency vehicle's open back door.

Everything was wet. Maybe the fire truck had sprayed the house and yard too. Tucker sat on a stretcher, quarreling with a petite female paramedic flanked by a larger male EMT. His hair appeared drenched too.

"There is nothing wrong with me. I need to go check on— *Sarah.*"

Their eyes met, and she almost collapsed to the damp, cold earth. *He's okay.* The female paramedic scowled at her before trailing the male paramedic to the ambulance, giving Sarah and Tucker privacy.

"Where's Onyx?" she asked.

He pointed behind him. The beautiful dog lay on his stomach in the open ambulance, nosing at the bandage on his front-left leg.

"What happened?" She took in every detail. A white bandage wrapped around Tucker's arm, and his shirt was removed, a brown blanket thrown over his shoulders in its place. She looked away from his bare chest, glueing her eyes to his dirt-streaked face instead. "Are you sure you're both all right?"

"It's just a superficial burn from the blast and there's a tiny cut from a piece of glass. See?" He held out one arm, and she stuffed down a sudden sob. He and Onyx could've been killed because of her. Because of these men after her.

She'd just lost Tanner, and while there was a long road ahead to process that grief, the thought of losing Tucker too, felt like being pounded with a tidal wave in the kiddie pool.

"Don't go there. This is *not* your fault."

It was disconcerting how easily he read her thoughts. She shook her head, pushing her hands into her jean's pockets. The air was bitterly cold now, with a dampness that permeated her skin. Her heart ached as she considered Liam. Was he comfortable, or hungry? Was he warm?

All she could cling to was a simple prayer —*God, bring him back to me, please*—and focus on the fact that Tucker and Onyx were safe.

The subject of her thoughts reached out, tucking a strand of hair clinging to her tearstained cheek behind her ear. His fingertips whispered across her skin, and she yearned to move closer. To lean into him. *Foolish thoughts*.

He drew his arm back under the blanket.

"What happened out here?" She motioned at the gaping hole where his door had been.

He shook his head, then pointed to his ear. "What?"

"What happened out here?" She repeated, then realized he was reading her lips. His hearing aid must've been damaged or dislodged. Tanner mentioned Tucker's hearing loss a long time ago, but he'd acted strange about it, so she'd never pressed for more information or asked what had happened.

"Two men. One must've started the fire, then the second came in and placed a bomb in the back door. Onyx let me know just in time."

"Were either of them caught?" She raised her voice over the rumbling fire truck and ambulance engines.

"Yes, Onyx helped me subdue one of the men. The suspect

has a substantial wound on his upper arm, so he was transported to Holloway General. We'll question him once he's out of surgery."

And maybe they'd get answers about Liam's whereabouts. "I'm sorry about the fire. And your door."

"I'm just grateful you and Onyx are safe."

"Hey, Tuck, you're cleared to go." The female paramedic edged between them to check the bandage on his arm. Her dark, curly hair was caught in a ponytail, and it bounced along with her impatient movements as she finished and packed up the medical gear. "You should probably go to the hospital just for good measure."

"Yeah, don't have time for that." He rammed a hand through his damp hair. "But thank you for gluing me back together again."

"You're a regular Humpty Dumpty," the paramedic teased, and Tucker gave her a lopsided grin. "I'm always available if you fall apart."

Sarah's eyes widened at the woman's bold words. There was no reason the EMT's interest in Tucker should bother her, but it did. She stepped over to Onyx, stroking the dog's head, and was rewarded with several licks to her hand.

"Poor, brave boy." She kissed the space between his ears, then turned when she heard Tucker's voice.

"Thanks, Marcy." He hopped off the stretcher, set the blanket down and gingerly pulled his tattered shirt back on. Then he came over to her, peering at Onyx's front leg.

"What happened?" she asked.

"Most likely a piece of wood or glass nicked his leg." He gently inspected the bandaged area, then scratched Onyx's neck. "I have a call in to his emergency vet. He should be able to take a look tonight."

"Will it keep him from working?"

"Not for long. These dogs are tough as nails." He turned his attention to her. "Your turn. Let's get you checked out."

She backed up. "I didn't get hurt. You made sure of that."

"Hey, I had to go through the medical rigmarole, so you do too."

Ten minutes later, after checking her blood pressure and putting a Band-Aid on a scratch on her ankle from the edge of the crawl space, Marcy noted with hooded eyes that Sarah was healthy and free to go.

"Thank you." She climbed off the stretcher. Marcy must consider her a threat. What a strange thought. Tucker wasn't interested in her. According to Tanner, Tucker had dated his high school girlfriend for two years. After she'd moved away and they'd broken up, Tucker still pined for her.

She caught her lower lip between her teeth as she considered the summer they first met. After Tucker had rescued her from the creek during that storm, he brought her back to the house he shared with his mom and Tanner. Then Tanner had entered the room like a whirlwind—like the storm had followed her into their house.

Tanner had been glued to her side the rest of the summer when she wasn't training in the pool, and she'd only seen Tucker a handful of times. He'd been friendly but distant. So quiet compared to Tanner's boisterousness. Once, she'd been at the house before Tanner arrived home, and she'd found Tucker in the backyard, shaping a rotted tree trunk into a small canoe. His methodical work with the carving knife had been mesmerizing, and she'd stayed out there for nearly an hour, watching and peppering him with questions before Tanner burst into the yard and demanded her attention again.

There hadn't been many other opportunities after that for one-on-one time with Tucker. In fact, looking back now, Sarah recognized that Tanner often wanted to hang out away from his house. Away from Tucker, who was working toward his degree in natural resources management while working in a volunteer position at the US Forest Service field office in Holloway.

A thought struck. "Did the fire damage anything in your garage?"

He turned, his handsome face weary under the glowing red police lights. "I haven't had a chance to look inside there yet. But my tools and carvings don't matter. You're safe. Onyx is safe. Now we focus on finding Liam. He matters, most of all."

The fierceness in Tucker's voice surprised her into silence. He waved at Heath, who had been circling the area around the barn door and was approaching them.

"Did you pray for rain?" Heath called out as he strode over. "Because you got it."

"Sure did." A wide smile softened Tucker's serious expression from moments ago.

"That's why you're all wet?" Her mouth went slack. "I figured you got sprayed by the fire hoses."

"Nah. God gave us ten minutes of rain to help put the fire out. Never doubt that He answers prayer." Tucker gazed at Sarah, seeming to see right into her heart in a way few others did. "That's why we keep praying for Liam. Never give up hope."

He turned and made his way toward the garage alongside Heath, and she ambled back over to Onyx, settling her fingers in his soft, thick fur. Her mind split in a dozen directions as she considered Liam's situation and Tucker's words.

Never doubt that He answers prayer.

Tucker's confidence bolstered her, and she prayed again for Liam's safe return. Hoped beyond hope that Tucker was right. While she was grateful they finally had one of the kidnappers in custody, she couldn't help but worry that the man wouldn't tell the police where her son was.

They were running out of time.

SIX

Tucker weaved through the piles of burnt wood in his garage. Only about half were damaged, and his mom's Civic was untouched other than ash on the windshield and one cracked window from the encroaching heat.

He kept picturing Sarah's expression of wonder after Heath mentioned the downpour that curtailed the last of the flames. He was fairly certain she wasn't a believer when they'd met years ago, and it had been another mark against his brother that Tanner, who had been raised in church and claimed Christ as his savior, hadn't continued going to church once they married.

At least, that's what his mom had said.

Did Sarah have faith in the Lord now?

He stepped around the blackened flooring, feeling along the Civic's sides and checking the tires. He would have to do better protecting himself from her. There was no guile in Sarah, and something about her always called to him. Did back then. Did now. And he needed to reinforce the armor around his heart to make sure she didn't get in there again.

No matter what, she'd always been Tanner's girl.

Tanner's quiet admission when he and Sarah became engaged still prodded Tucker's heart.

Sarah commented about your hearing aid. She thinks it's

weird. Said she gets frustrated talking to you because she has to repeat herself. I'd just avoid her if I were you.

His jaw ticked as he rejoined Heath outside. Almost ten years later, the words still stung. After one last quick sweep of the interior and exterior of the garage, he returned to the ambulance to find Heath speaking with Sarah. He exhaled harshly and shook off the hurt from the past. *Did* she think his hearing aid was weird?

Heath crossed his arms. "You sure you don't need to go to the hospital? Just for old time's sake?" His friend jabbed his ribs, and Tucker shot him a *Watch it* look. Heath was likely referring to the two cybercriminals who had jumped him at the ranger station months ago.

"I'm good, man. Drop it."

Heath held out his palms. "Okay, okay. You want to tell me what happened?"

Tucker recounted the evening's events in quick succession, including hiding Sarah in the crawl space. Heath's brows shot up as Tucker relayed Onyx whining about the pack, giving them just enough of a head start to get away from the explosion.

"My officers have taken pictures, and they're collecting evidence. Looks like it was a basic pipe bomb. Small. Homemade."

"I wonder if it was meant to distract me rather than kill anyone."

"You think this was all to get to Sarah?" Heath asked.

"I'm starting to. Maybe they wanted her but grabbed Liam instead because she put up such a big fight when they tried to nab her." Tucker scrubbed a palm over his eyes. "Were you able to get Tanner's cell phone from her car at the cottage?"

"I was about to send an officer out there when we got your call. We'll retrieve it in the morning." Heath's phone buzzed.

"Hold on a sec." He read something on the screen, then reread it, his eyes widening.

Tucker's stomach jumped. "What is it?"

"A large, gray cat was found wandering Route 6. Collar and tag matches Sarah's son's cat. Because we had it listed on the missing person's report, a local citizen remembered the description and called it in."

"They found Mr. Meow? What about Liam?"

"No sign of the kidnapper's vehicle or any other items left behind. No Liam. The cat is at the vet, the same one you take Onyx to. We're checking the area."

Tucker tapped a fist to his chin. What a mixed bag of news. "Too bad we can't get prints off feline fur."

"Right. Same thought crossed my mind. We'll work on Suspect A here once he's out of surgery tomorrow."

While Tucker was relieved to get the cat back, too many questions remained about Liam. Was he still in the area? Had the kidnappers taken him back to Fountain View? Would the men send a ransom note—and how?

"I need to bring Onyx to the vet tonight. Dr. Gill texted me back, said he'd come in and take a look at the wound."

"That's good. Have her verify it's the right cat too. Listen, this place is a mess, man," Heath noted grimly. "You're both welcome to stay at my house."

Tucker sighed. Heath was right. There was a small sleeping area above his garage, and while it hadn't been damaged by the fire, it would likely reek of smoke. He wasn't even sure the building was still structurally sound. His engineer friend, Ken, would have to do an inspection of the garage and the house.

"Thanks for the offer. I'll let Sarah know. After I take Onyx to the vet and see about the cat, I'll head to your place so we can get some rest."

Sarah sidled up next to Tucker, her elbow pressing into his arm. "Any news about Liam?"

"Unfortunately, no, but we did locate your son's cat," Heath answered.

"You found Mr. Meow?" Myriad emotions flooded her face. Relief, joy, confusion. Then it clouded over again. "Where?"

"On Route 6," Tucker answered. "He's at the same vet's office where I'll be taking Onyx."

"Is he okay?"

"The cat appears to be unhurt," Heath replied slowly. "We believe the men ditched him after they...after Liam was taken."

"Can I get him?"

He and Heath exchanged a look before Tucker answered. "I think the vet will want to keep him overnight for observation. Confirm he's not injured. Also, we believe it's safest for you to stay at Heath's house."

"Where will you be?" she asked Tucker.

"I'll stay there as well, after I drop off Onyx. He won't like it, but he'll be at the vet's overnight too."

Ten minutes later, after checking his Bronco's engine, tires, and undercarriage for anything tampered with or cut, Tucker, Sarah and Onyx drove back down Tucker's driveway toward Holloway.

Sarah was quiet for several minutes as they left the house behind and the forest enveloped them. He was lost in his thoughts about his house damage and how to break the news to his mom about Tanner and Liam tomorrow when he noticed her swiping at her cheeks.

"Sarah?"

"You could've been killed." Her voice sounded small and faraway.

"I wasn't, so there's no reason to keep thinking about that. Onyx and I are fine."

"But your house. It's damaged, and you can't stay there."

"It's fixable. Plus, Heath's house is always open and Piper—his daughter—loves company. She calls me Uncle Tuck." Always an uncle—would he ever be a father? He swallowed and continued. "Onyx knows his two dogs, and they get along great. Dogpile and all." He chuckled, but the sound felt as rough as rocks.

She sniffled, and he laid a hand on her forearm, sending a jolt through his skin. "Now that we've caught one of them, we'll pray it leads to more information on who these criminals are, who they're working for, and what they want from you."

Tucker gnawed the inside of his cheek. He had a feeling tonight's events were a ruse to try to kidnap Sarah too. They must want something from her—but what?

He prayed their reasoning became clear after Holloway PD interviewed the suspect. He and Heath had to stay one step ahead of them—to locate Liam and keep Sarah safe.

Before it was too late.

Sarah curled her fingers into the seatbelt as Tucker drove toward Heath's house. For the thousandth time that evening, her thoughts returned to Liam. If he couldn't sleep tonight, his anxiety would be even worse tomorrow. Did he have a blanket? Was he warm and fed? He was probably worried about Mr. Meow's whereabouts. While he was mostly well-behaved, under these circumstances, no child would exhibit normal behavior. Tears stung her eyes, so she closed them.

Please, God. I'm trying to have faith. You answered Tucker's prayer and gave him rain. Please, please bring my son back to me.

Tucker clicked on the turning signal. "Listen, about your friend's husband. Officer Drew Stevens. He's a trustworthy guy?"

"I think so. I've known Amy, his wife, for years. She swam the butterfly leg of our relay at the Games, and I was a bridesmaid in their wedding. Drew has won awards in the community. He's a good guy." It hit her that Drew, with his quiet attentiveness and steadfast care for Amy, reminded her of Tucker.

"Let's hope your instincts are correct."

"Why do you say that?"

"Because either the men who killed Tanner followed you here, or they were tipped off by someone. I hope it's the first."

"I can't believe Drew would betray me. He was very patient about Tanner's death and accommodating about meeting me at our house before we left town."

"Did you give him permission to check your house?"

She closed her eyes and rubbed her fingertips over her eyelids. "I can't remember. Maybe?"

"Heath and I will give him a call later today, and I'm hoping he'll send us what he's gathered on the investigation so far. By then we'll have Tanner's cell phone."

Speaking of which, she hadn't checked hers in a while. Sarah pulled her cell from her purse. The screen flashed, highlighting missed calls and more messages. She put in her passcode and checked voicemail. *Four* messages?

The most recent one was from Liam's teacher, letting her know his cookie order was ready for pickup. They were part of a holiday fundraiser for his class. The second and third were from Amy via Drew, and Sarah had already listened to them.

Sarah tapped the fourth message and played it on speaker.

"Sarah, this is Alexander Drake. Please call me. I'm at the Fountain View police station talking to authorities. Something happened at work. I need to speak to you."

She clicked out of her messages and clutched her phone. Tucker shot her a speculative look. "Who's that?"

"Alexander is the CEO of Zeta Pharmaceuticals. I realize I should've mentioned him before."

"Do you trust *him*?" Tucker echoed the same question he asked moments ago about Drew.

She tilted her head back. "Right off the bat, I would say yes, but so much has happened in the last twenty-four hours that I never thought would happen. And I don't know Mr. Drake that well. I guess it's possible, especially since Tanner and Mr. Drake didn't see eye to eye lately. Obviously, Alexander had a huge stake in this medication going to market. It would've been a windfall for Zeta Pharmaceuticals."

"I'd like to— Whoa!"

Tucker jerked the wheel just as a powerful impact from behind spun his Bronco in circles. Sarah screamed, and their dark surroundings whirled by as though they were caught in a tornado. The road beneath the Bronco's tires suddenly changed from concrete to spongy dirt, and the sharp crack of sticks and branches resounded as they careened onto the shoulder.

He wrestled with the steering wheel, engaging the brake so the spin slowed. Another hard *thud* to the side of the SUV changed their trajectory, wringing a gasp from Sarah. Onyx yelped from the back seat, and her right arm jammed against the passenger door as the vehicle slid farther away from the roadside. She looked around, her chest heaving. They'd ended up several feet down an embankment, inside the tree line.

Darkness covered them like a black cloak the instant they stopped spinning. Only the Bronco's headlights pierced the dark, highlighting the thick forest around them. Tucker lay deathly still, his forehead resting awkwardly on the steering wheel.

"Tucker?" She reached over, gently touched the side of his face. He was breathing, but his body was limp. The second hit must have knocked him out.

Onyx whined behind her, and she turned to find the dog sitting in the middle of the seat, his harness intact. She reached back and released the harness. The dog wriggled out of it, then stood in between the two front seats, nosing Tucker.

"He's okay, boy. Easy. We need to call for help." She reached for her cell, but the powerful force of the crash had slung it somewhere. Under a seat. In the back?

A man's voice carried over, and a single beam of light invaded the Bronco's interior. Their pursuer was out of his car. Coming for them. For her.

She made sure the door locks were engaged. But Tucker was out cold. She couldn't run away and leave him. Plus, she had Onyx. *The gun*. Where did he keep his gun?

She froze when the male voice closed in. Tremors tore over her limbs as the feeling of being cornered overwhelmed her.

A sharp, slicing sound bounced off the inside of Tucker's vehicle. She turned to find the tip of a knife poked through the canvas top of the Bronco, in the back near the trunk. Someone was slitting through the top rather than attempting to open the door.

A low, rumbling growl began in Onyx's throat, barely audible over the cutting sound and the attacker's heavy breathing. The man started a second slit, then connected them in order to create a larger opening.

A dozen thoughts crisscrossed her mind. What command should she give the dog? Onyx had the advantage of surprise, but she hated for him to get hurt. Tucker loved him so much.

Due to the shadowy night and the dark canvas material and windows, their attacker must not realize there was a K9 in the car. She reached for the flashlight in the glove box and set her finger on the on/off switch. Turning it on would blind the man when he tried to get inside the trunk area behind the back seat. She had to help Onyx in any way she could.

"Shh," she told the dog as the man's arm pushed through the hole, enlarging it. "Wait, boy. Hold."

Onyx quietly manipulated his agile frame so he was facing backward, watching the person tearing through the Bronco's canvas. His muscular chest and hind legs trembled, the black fur shimmering. Tucker moaned and moved his head, but the moan was covered by the sound of the knife piercing the canvas top once more. Four holes, then the man grabbed the loose material and ripped it downward.

The opening was wide enough for a man's shoulder now. Her stomach twisted as the attacker shoved his entire arm and part of his chest into the vehicle, blindly reaching for the back door locks.

Onyx launched silently over the back seat, his powerful jaws closing over the man's upper arm. The intruder's guttural cry of pain screamed through the vehicle, and Tucker startled awake with a shout.

"Tucker?" She stroked his neck as he struggled to straighten in the seat. "Please, wake up."

Tucker rammed the heel of his hand into his forehead, and his eyes rolled around wildly at the ruckus behind him. He reached to his side and tugged out his weapon. When he lay the gun on his lap, then grabbed her hand and put it on the weapon, all the air in her lungs whooshed out.

"Aim out the window," he mumbled in between the man's howling. "I c-can't focus. You may...have to shoot the intruder."

"I might accidentally shoot Onyx."

Their pursuer flung his arm around, shouting and cursing as he attempted to disengage Onyx's hold. A halo of red circled the spot on his arm where Onyx held on.

"You can do this," Tucker urged. "Steady."

Sarah clasped the gun, then aimed at the back driver-side

door. How could she do this with her hands so shaky? And what if she killed him? Especially since this man probably knew where Liam was.

"Wait. Onyx, release." His voice was weak. "Release!" he repeated, louder.

Onyx let go of the man's arm, and the assailant howled and disappeared from view. His uneven footsteps thudded into the night. Seconds later a car engine started up, and it revved then sped away. Sarah set the gun on the console then sagged against the seat, her limbs trembling.

"Can you call…?" He asked.

"My phone fell. Let me find it." She reached down to the floorboards, feeling around in the dark, as Tucker slowly turned to croon at Onyx. The dog panted heavily in the back, gusts of his breath clouding the rapidly cooling vehicle.

The crunch of gravel alerted them to the arrival of another car, and then a door slammed shut. Two beams of bright lights sliced through the Bronco from behind.

Sarah's breath froze in her chest as wintery air seeped into the vehicle. Who had arrived now?

SEVEN

"Tuck, you all right?"

Tucker squinted into the flashlight's blinding beam, sending a sharp jab of pain through his skull. Heath.

"Hey, man, turn that off." He shifted in his seat, facing Sarah so he could use his good ear and meeting her rounded eyes. "What happened after we got run off the road?"

"The guy cut into the back of your car, and Onyx got him by the arm." She grimaced. "It was bad. There's blood all over the place."

"You're not hurt?" Tucker asked.

She shook her head, their gazes clinging.

He turned to survey his brave partner. The dog was still panting, and he gingerly reached back to check Onyx's frame for wounds. The wrap on the dog's front leg had slipped lower, but under the Bronco's dim dome light, it appeared that no blood had seeped out.

Tucker pivoted and met Heath's gaze. "Did you get a look at the car that hit us?"

"He was gone by the time I got here. Onyx bit his arm?" Heath asked Sarah.

She cringed. "For sure. He had a good hold on him."

"Okay, I'll put out an APB, mention the arm wound. If he

stays in the area, he may hit up a doctor's office or walk-in clinic tonight or tomorrow."

Heath stepped back as Tucker slowly climbed out of his Bronco. Sarah exited through her door and hurried around, offering her arm for Tucker to steady himself.

"I was about five minutes behind you. What happened?"

Tucker settled his backside against the Bronco's front wheel well as he explained. "I didn't even get a look at the vehicle."

Heath pointed at Tucker's head. "You need to go get that checked out. Sarah should go too, just in case."

"I'm fine," she replied. "But I'll go so...so I can stay with Tucker in case we need to communicate about what happened."

Sirens blared as a second Holloway squad car arrived, lights flashing as it parked. Two men climbed out, Officer Anthony Venetta and a new officer Tucker didn't recognize.

Heath briefed them, then the officers began checking for tire tracks and casing the crash site.

"I need to get Onyx to the vet." Tucker opened the back driver-side door. Onyx sat on his haunches, still panting but alert. Tucker pulled out a half-frozen bottle of water and poured it in the dog's travel bowl, letting Onyx drink for several seconds. Then he retrieved Jerry and tossed the stuffed animal at his partner. Onyx seized Jerry and lay back on the seat, the mangled giraffe caught fast between his paws.

"He seems good, but I still want him checked out in case there are any internal issues."

"Sure thing," Heath responded. "I'll set up a tow for this once the officers are done checking for blood samples, then I'll take you two—you three," he corrected himself, "to the vet, then the hospital."

"See if Roger Buchanan's shop can take this, would you?" Tucker asked.

Forty-five minutes later Tucker lay on a hospital bed in Holloway General. They had dropped Onyx off at the vet's office first, given the overnight tech a rundown of what had happened, Sarah had checked to make sure the cat they'd found was Mr. Meow and then they'd headed to the hospital next. Heath had left Tucker and Sarah at the hospital's front doors to return to the Bronco and help with the investigation. Sarah would pick up Mr. Meow once they left the hospital.

Tucker's head throbbed as he mentally ran through the events of the evening. The fire, then getting run off the road. It all blurred now from the lack of sleep and the crash. Sarah sat in a chair beside him, tapping away on her cell.

"There." She set the phone on her lap. "I texted Alexander Drake back."

"Tanner's boss, right?"

"Yes. The Zeta CEO. He flew back into the country and just gave his statement to officers in Fountain View."

Tucker closed his eyes and set the heel of his hand on his brow. When he opened them and turned his head, he caught Sarah watching him, concern etched on her lovely face. Her long blond hair fell in disarray around her shoulders, and he forced his gaze away. Even worried, tired after fighting for her life, and missing her son, she was the most beautiful woman he'd ever seen.

And she'd chosen Tanner. *Don't forget that.*

"Tucker?" she asked. "Should I call a doctor?"

"No, I'm just thinking about Tanner." He adjusted his frame in the uncomfortable bed. "I still can't believe he's gone."

"Me either." Her eyes clouded over, and her gaze fell.

Theirs didn't sound like an ideal marriage, but Tucker wouldn't bad-mouth his brother. He and Tanner rarely had seen eye to eye on things, but now that he was dead... He swallowed, his throat tight. *What I wouldn't give to talk to you one more time, brother. Tell you none of those stupid childish arguments matter. But I can't. I can promise I'll find your son.*

And I'll keep Sarah safe.

And that was it. He was Sarah's protector, nothing more. She'd made that clear when they were younger, both by her actions in choosing Tanner and by what she'd told Tanner about Tucker's hearing loss. While he didn't enjoy having to use a hearing aid, it was part of him. Part of who he was—a part she didn't like.

Time to move on to another subject.

"The drug Tanner was working on—what's it called?"

"Nuexta."

"Did Alexander Drake and Tanner argue about Nuexta or the clinical trials for it?"

"I'm not sure. Tanner was on calls all the time when he worked from home. I do know that things were tense between him and several people from Zeta the last month especially. Alexander Drake could have been one of them."

"Tanner didn't share his concerns about any of this?"

"He would make comments once in a while, but most of the time he kept it quiet. Maybe because he didn't want me knowing your mom was involved in the trial?" She paused, sighing. "Also, Liam was usually around, and I had made it clear that Tanner wasn't to bring up a lot of negative things around him."

He could practically see the weight return to her shoulders at the mention of her son. A change of topic was in order. "How's it going with your swim team and the lessons?"

Another sigh, and Tucker scowled. *Whoops*.

"It's been a rough year. My assistant coach left to start another swim club in north Philly, and several families followed him. Amy, Drew Stevens's wife, has been helping coach. As far as my swim-lesson business, with it being winter, the number of appointments drops. It's slow season."

"Do you mind me asking what happened with the other coach?"

"Tom and I had different visions for the team. I believe under-twelves should be building endurance and improving stroke technique *and* having fun; he thinks they're training for the Junior Olympics. I like the kids to have silly relay days on Fridays, but Tom thought it was a waste of two hours that could be used for serious training."

"I'd rather have my kids on your team."

A tiny smile appeared. "Thanks. I had a few parents say the same thing, which is why seventeen families stuck around. Liam started swimming this summer too, but I'm not sure how long that will last." Her smile rose then faltered. "He loves—loved—the relay days. For one of the races, the kids get to wear their flip flops or Crocs while swimming. He thought that was so funny."

He reached over to pat her arm. "We're getting closer to finding him."

The door swung open, and a nurse trotted in. Tucker withdrew his hand as the woman addressed him.

"Hello. Dr. Swett viewed your tests. Everything looks a-okay. He cleared you to leave once the paperwork is finished, but he does recommend you get some rest."

"I'll try." He'd rest once they found Liam.

Sarah cleared her throat and, after the nurse slipped back through the door, said, "When did the vet say Onyx would be able to go home?"

"He wasn't sure. Hopefully tomorrow."

"You're very attached to him," she observed.

"When he and I trained together a couple months ago after his handler's death, we hit it off. He's smart, focused, hard-working, and a bit stubborn." He chuckled. "My supervisor thought this type of work may be a better fit for Onyx. My job is physical, and he has as much restless energy as I do."

Her cell buzzed. "It's Mr. Drake."

"You should probably answer it."

She tapped the green button. "Mr. Drake, hello." Then she clicked the speaker button so Tucker could hear the conversation as well. "You've given your statement?"

"I did. Rita spoke with the officer as well."

Sarah frowned, and her eyes caught on Tucker's. "Your wife needed to speak to them as well?"

"She had to confirm we were out of the country. For investigative purposes. Now, what is going on at your end? Did I hear right that your son is missing?" Mr. Drake's voice dripped with concern, but Tucker didn't know him well enough to gauge authenticity.

Sarah's chest rose and fell. "Yes. Liam was kidnapped."

Tucker vigorously shook his head, mouthing the words, *Don't share much.*

"Sarah, I am so sorry. What a terrible loss for you, and now this. I hope you'll accept my deepest condolences."

"Thank you. It's been a difficult couple of days."

"Do they know who kidnapped him? Any leads?"

Again, Tucker shook his head.

"I… I'm not sure."

"I do hope they find him." Mr. Drake exhaled. "There is one other aspect about Tanner's situation I wanted to discuss with you." He paused, the silence weighty. "Do you remember Mark Sousa?"

Tucker held out both hands in a *stop* gesture. He shook his head, and his headache split across his skull.

"Barely." She gnawed on her lip, clearly uncomfortable with the lie. "But it's late and I'm tired. He works at Zeta too?"

"He does. He's a research scientist. I was just curious if you knew about Tanner's relationship with Mark. The police are trying to locate Mark to bring him in for questioning."

"I'm sorry, Mr. Drake. I may have heard Tanner mention him, but my brain is all scrambled right now."

Tucker gave her a thumbs-up.

"Listen, I don't want to keep you," Mr. Drake said. "I need to get some rest as well. We had a long day of travel. Maybe we can discuss this later in the day today? Oh, and Sarah?"

The way Mr. Drake said her name sent a chill down Tucker's spine.

"Yes?" Her shoulders curled forward.

"Please be careful out there. It's possible Tanner, and Mark, were involved in a dangerous situation, and I'm determined to get to the bottom of it. I will not allow Zeta Pharmaceuticals to be dragged through the mud from this."

"I will. Good night." She ended the call and fell back in the chair.

"We need to find out what exactly he means by all that," Tucker noted. Mark Sousa was apparently missing. Tucker would let Heath know, and Heath needed to confirm this news with Officer Stevens in Fountain View.

Just then, the nurse burst back through the door. "Discharge paperwork. You're a free bird, Mr. Brindley."

Tucker rose cautiously from the hospital bed, feeling incapable of flying at the moment. Instead, he limped through the room, his thoughts circling back to Mr. Drake's last few words to Sarah. A warning?

It's possible Tanner, and Mark, were involved in a dangerous situation... I will not allow Zeta Pharmaceuticals to be dragged through the mud from this...

Sarah stood beside Tucker at Heath's front door. He had scoped out the yard and street before they exited their police car ride, and then they'd dragged themselves up the front walk. It was early in the morning, and she hoped they wouldn't wake up Heath's daughter when they entered.

Heath met them at the front door wearing Snoopy pajamas and a rumpled gray T-shirt that read *World's Best Dad*. Two dogs circled his feet, pressing their noses into Tucker's and Sarah's legs.

"Don't be nervous around these two," Heath said, noting her hesitation. "This is Axel, and this guy's Forge. If you're friends with me, they're friends with you. Plus, you're female. They like females." He grinned.

She reached down to pet them, noting Tucker's low-key demeanor as he stroked the dogs' ears. Did he miss Onyx?

Mr. Meow and Onyx would remain at the vet's office until morning. She couldn't wait to pick up Mr. Meow, although part of her was torn because it was just the cat.

Not Liam.

They shuffled into the house, the same prayer filling her mind. *Please, God, bring him back to me safe.*

Heath locked the door, then set his alarm. Both dogs followed as he led Sarah and Tucker to the living room. A majestic Christmas tree filled the corner, beautiful but bare except for lights.

"We haven't finished decorating the tree yet. Piper's about ready to do it herself." He chuckled, then gestured from Tucker to the couch. "You mind sleeping here?"

"It's all good. I'm zonked."

Heath turned to Sarah, his voice a low whisper. "There's a double bed in the guest room upstairs. Some of my sister Katie's stuff is still up there. You can just put it on the recliner beside the window. She watches Piper when I get called into work."

He rammed a hand through his hair, and curiosity bubbled over. Where was his wife?

"Piper is asleep and I'd rather not wake her," Heath continued. "When she doesn't sleep, her crabby-cakes side comes out."

"I'll be quiet. Liam gets the same way. Kids need their sleep." She yawned. "I appreciate you taking me—us—in like this." She glanced at Tucker and found him watching them with a brooding expression.

"Of course. There's a bathroom upstairs. I put out an extra towel if you need it. I'm heading to bed, or else there'll be two crabby cakes tomorrow. Help yourselves to whatever you need in the fridge or pantry. Also, tomorrow you're welcome to use my w—the extra car in the garage." His gaze fell to the floor.

"Thanks, Heath," Tucker responded. "Good night."

"Night." Heath headed into a room tucked just past the stairs. The clickety-clack of the dogs' claws filled the quiet house as they followed him. One climbed the stairs while the other disappeared in Heath's room.

"Did I miss something?" she asked. "He seemed…sad."

Tucker's mouth turned down. "The extra car is his deceased wife's. She passed a couple years ago."

"Oh, how sad." So that was why his sister watched Piper. "Were they…was it a happy marriage?"

"Yeah, it was. They really had each other's backs, you know? Seeing them together gave me hope."

"Hope?"

"That there are healthy, stable relationships out there. People who commit to the 'to love and cherish, in sickness and in health, until death do us part' line and mean it."

"I believed in that at one time too." She was so tired she spoke without any forethought.

Tucker shook his head. "He really hurt you, didn't he?" He

clasped her elbow and led her to the couch, then they sank down, side by side. A wall clock ticked off the relentless march of time, much like her heavy heartbeat.

She knew he meant Tanner without speaking her husband's name. But she wouldn't disparage him, especially now that he was dead.

"We...both hurt each other. It wasn't just him." Her words trailed off as tears and memories circled her throat.

"Tanner is gone, Sarah. You don't have to pretend he lived a perfect life. None of us do. If you need to talk, or vent, or just cry, I'm here."

"Right now, I just miss Liam. So much I physically hurt. For a minute I forget he's gone, then I remember again, and I feel horrible that I forgot." She covered her face with both hands, and he settled an arm around her. "What if he's cold? Or hungry? Or hurt?" She sobbed. "I can't stand the thought of him scared. All alone."

She collapsed into him, and he held her close as she cried.

"I want them to take me. Just take me!" Another sob shook her. "Leave Liam alone."

After a few moments and too many tears to count, Tucker cleared his throat. "I'd like to pray for him, if that's all right?"

"Yes. Please," she practically begged, swiping at her eyes and nose. He reached over to the coffee table and handed her a tissue box, and she withdrew several, crushing them in her palm as Tucker prayed.

"Dear Lord, please comfort Sarah. She loves her son so much and wants him back safely. You know all about that because You gave us Jesus, and You loved him so much. But You still gave Him as a sacrifice for our sins." Tucker paused and cleared his throat again. "We pray You would protect Liam, keep him safe and warm, and that tomorrow You would lead the officers and myself to find him. Please also help Sarah get some rest tonight. In Jesus's name, amen."

"Amen," she murmured. "Thank you, Tucker. You've been a rock for me since this all started. You and Onyx. I don't know what I'd be doing or what would've happened if…"

"I believe God put me near your cottage at the right time to help you. I'm not normally in that area at night." He set his cheek to her hair, and the scent of pine and fresh air calmed her. "Anytime you need me, I'll be there."

"Sometimes I think about that summer…" she began, then stopped as the words jammed up in her throat like Liam's classmates in line on the way to the school lunchroom. "And I wonder why you and I didn't talk more."

"Because my brother drew an invisible line around you."

She frowned. "What do you mean?"

"Tanner claimed you as his, and he didn't like sharing." Tucker carefully disengaged his arm then stood. "And because he was the one you wanted to spend time with, not me."

She blinked up at him. Was he…upset? Was it possible Tucker would've been interested in her? What if—

"Would you like something to drink or eat?" He interrupted the questions rising in her mind.

She rose and followed him, heat climbing her throat. "Just a water, please."

He opened the fridge and handed her a bottle, his gaze finally connecting with hers. "You better get upstairs. It'll be morning soon."

"Yeah. Thank you again for praying for Liam." Then she turned around and climbed the stairs before she could read too much into the protective mask that dropped over his face when he'd said *because he was the one you wanted to spend time with, not me.*

Getting her son back was the most important matter to

focus on. Questioning her and Tucker's past accomplished nothing except to heap on more self-doubt and uncertainty.

It was best to let the past stay the past.

EIGHT

Sarah followed Tucker into Holloway Animal Hospital at nine the next morning. She shivered as a sharp gust of winter wind chased them in, lifting her hair like an invisible hand and making her glance backward with a jolt.

Would she always be looking around, checking her back?

Mr. Meow's faint, plaintive mewls carried down the hallway, and her heart tripped. *Poor boy. I'm coming for you.*

She hurried to keep up with Tucker's long, determined strides. It was evident he missed his partner too. He bypassed the reception desk and several occupied chairs, giving a brief wave to a red-haired woman speaking on the phone. The woman waved back, and Sarah offered a weak smile. An enthusiastic yellow Lab whined from the visitor lobby, jumping up and tugging on its leash when they walked past.

She stifled a yawn. Though she'd slept some last night, it was barely enough to function at 8:00 a.m., when Tucker and Heath's rumbling voices had woken her. After cleaning herself up, she'd joined them for blueberry waffles while trying not to cry into the syrup as she wondered what Liam was eating. *If* he was eating. He loved blueberry waffles. How could she eat if she wasn't sure her son was being fed? The food had tasted like cardboard, but she'd forced it down at Tucker's urging.

He'd acted normal this morning, no trace of the awkwardness between them after she'd brought up their complicated shared history. She trailed him down the veterinary office corridor, noting three doors on each side. After passing those and a sign that read *Employees Only*, they reached another door—a swinging one with no lock. They pushed through and entered a long, white-washed room packed with crates, several exam tables and dozens of cabinets. As soon as they stepped inside, a cacophony of whines, barking and meowing exploded.

"Whoa. Full house, Doc?" Tucker addressed a sandy-haired man on the far side of the room tending to a wiggly beagle with a cone around its plump neck.

"Full as ever." The veterinarian turned, a friendly smile on his bearded face. His voice carried a subtle Australian accent. "With the holiday coming, we're fully booked with boarders."

"Sounds that way." Tucker turned to her. "Sarah, this is Dr. Gill. Oliver, this is Sarah...Brindley."

The doctor's light brown brows arched. "Sister-in-law or speed-dating experience?" he quipped, and Sarah's mouth dropped open.

"Tanner's wife," Tucker answered brusquely, and the vet made an *oops* face. "She's...an old friend."

"Right-o. So, your fella is over there." Dr. Gill pointed to the corner, where Onyx's black nose pressed against a massive wire crate. The *whomp, whomp* of his tail increased as Tucker strode over. "And the cat we got in last night is up there."

Sarah beelined for the small wire crate situated on the top shelf. She glanced at the doctor. "Is he okay?"

"Right as rain. You know cats, they always land on their feet."

Sarah opened the latch and cooed to Mr. Meow, whose large frame filled half the crate. "My poor kitty, what happened?" *Where is your boy?* she almost asked aloud.

"I took off the collar he was wearing. It's right big, and

I wanted to get a look at his throat. The feline's in excellent health." The vet addressed Tucker. "Now, for your brave pup, I cleaned the wound. It's small, not too deep. Didn't need stitches. Just watch him that he doesn't chew on the area. Cone of shame if he does. Nancy has some pain meds and an antibiotic for him up front when you leave. A cone, too, in case the need arises. Also, the cat's collar is in a bag up front."

"Do you think it's best that Onyx is off duty for a while?" Tucker inquired.

"He's fit, no doubt about that, but don't overdo it. I'm more concerned about the chewing."

Ten minutes later Tucker and Sarah loaded the two animals into the older model SUV Heath lent them. Dr. Gill had offered to let her borrow the carrier for Mr. Meow for now, and she set it on the back seat beside Onyx in his harness. Tucker scratched the dog's neck and ears and stroked his deep chest while murmuring to him in a funny, singsong voice.

The deep bond between the two warmed her despite the chilly air.

"We need to go to the station to give our statements. Onyx will be fine with me, but I'm wondering where we should leave the cat." He motioned to the carrier, and, as if on cue, Mr. Meow mewled unhappily. "He would be thrilled to be out of the container and—"

"Tucker, I just realized Mr. Meow's litter box is at the cottage. It's a little travel one. He'll need it."

"I have to stop and grab some can food for Onyx. The store should have litter boxes too."

Halfway there, a call came in on Tucker's phone.

"Heath. What's up?"

"Suspect one is going in for surgery in an hour. Ten-thirty. The doctor says it may be late this afternoon or tonight before we can speak to him."

"And even then, he'll be coming out of anesthesia."

"Exactly." Heath's frustrated voice mirrored Tucker's.

"Any news about Tanner's cell phone?"

"Unfortunately, I haven't had the manpower to send someone to the cottage to retrieve that. We're still going over your property for evidence and finishing up with the prints on your Bronco."

Tucker pulled into the Tops Grocery store parking lot, near Watley Industries, a huge equipment manufacturing plant. He ended the call, then turned to her. "Let's go in together."

Sarah cooed to Mr. Meow once more then they locked the vehicle and walked inside the store. It was cool outside but not freezing, so the animals would be fine in the car for five minutes. She grabbed a cart as they made their way inside.

Tucker motioned to the left. "The pet food aisle is—"

"Tucker Brindley! Just the young man I wanted to see." The wizened voice of an older woman caught them like a snare, and he muffled a groan.

"Mrs. Haggerty. How are you?" He turned as a short, heavyset woman beelined out of the canned-vegetable aisle. Straight toward them. Tucker's body language wasn't difficult to read—he would've avoided the approaching woman if he could, but there was no place to hide. Sarah planted on an uncertain smile as Tucker held out his hands then was dragged into a ferocious, slightly awkward hug.

"Where is your handsome partner?" The woman—Mrs. Haggerty—pulled back, an eager grin lifting her cheeks.

"He's waiting in the car."

"Oh, give that good boy my love and an extra treat." The woman peered around Tucker, eyes alighting on Sarah. "And *who* is this?"

"Sarah, this is Rose Haggerty. Rose is one of my mom's former coworkers at Holloway Elementary and a family friend."

"You didn't answer my question." Rose winked conspiratorially at Sarah.

"Sarah is...she's a friend."

"Just a friend? Do young people take their *friends* shopping nowadays?" Another wink. "It's about time you get hitched, young man."

Warmth inched up Sarah's neck. What a sweet but obnoxious woman. The perils of small towns were that you were guaranteed to run into people you knew at the store.

"It's so nice to meet you, Rose," she said, then met Tucker's chagrinned expression. "Tucker, how about I go find the litter box while you two catch up?"

He wagged his brows at her in apology. "Sounds good. I'll be right there."

"Nice to meet you," she said as she pushed the cart away.

Sarah is... She's a friend. Surely they *were* friends, especially after the terrible situation with Liam and Tanner. But... was that how Tucker had always viewed her?

She shook off the turn of her thoughts and headed down the pet-food aisle, which was situated on the other end of the grocery store. Her limbs felt listless, and it was an effort to walk in a straight line as her eyes roved the shelves. There. Litter and litter boxes.

She chose the smallest litter box and placed it in the cart along with a container of litter, then turned and focused on canned dog food. Did Tucker have a specific brand he bought?

A figure caught her attention from the corner of her eye. Sarah's muscles quivered as a slender man of average height dressed in camo pants and a dark shirt turned the corner and started down the same aisle, but from the opposite end she'd used. A black ballcap rode low on his head, obscuring his eyes and part of his nose. Her pulse skipped into overdrive.

It's probably just another shopper. Still, the sensation of being watched—being targeted—tweaked her nerves.

Should she shout for Tucker? No. There was no danger. Just a hunch. Sarah tugged out her cell and put it to her ear, then began talking animatedly. "Yes, Mom, I'll be over soon. I'll bring something for us to eat." She paused in the fake conversation, sadness tripping her up. Her mom had died of a drug overdose a few years ago. What she wouldn't give to speak to her Mom again. "Okay, I'll see you soon. Love you too."

She pretended to end the call, her throat thickening as she imagined actually calling her mom and speaking like this to her. Instead, she drew in a deep breath and willed herself not to stare as the man approached her.

He slowed his cart a few feet away, then caught her watching him. Had he even looked at anything on the shelves? Chills slithered over her as a sneering smile creased his face. A scar marked his cheek, ugly and puckered.

"Now, now, Sarah. Don't lie. Your mom isn't alive anymore." He shoved his cart at hers, knocking her backward into a stack of canned dog food. Several toppled over, and she jerked away to keep her cart between herself and the man and to avoid getting hit on the head by the heavy cans.

"Tucker! Help!"

"Did you get my note?" the man snarled, then he abandoned his cart and retraced the path he'd come. Toward the meat section in the back of the store.

"Where is my son?" she shouted after him, her heart thundering in her chest. Then she sank to the floor. Where was Liam? What note did he mean?

"Sarah!" Tucker flew across the grocery store's main aisle, toward the pet food. He never should have let her out of his sight.

Several customers gaped at him as he weaved through carts filled with holiday food. "Law enforcement. Stay back." He met one of the cashier's wide-eyed gazes. "Call 9-1-1."

There she was. Relief burned through his veins. Sarah was huddled three-quarters of the way down the aisle, crumpled against a small mountain of displaced canned food. A cart filled with a plastic litter box and a container of litter sat askew. She struggled upright and rushed forward, falling into his embrace. Clinging tightly.

As much as he wished he could stay like this forever, he had to catch the criminal who had hurt her and abducted Liam. He pulled away. "What happened?"

"A man came from there—" she motioned to the back of the aisle "—and walked toward me. He was watching me too. I pretended to call my mom and talk to her, but…" She hiccupped on a sob.

"But what?" Tucker was pretty sure her mom was deceased.

"He said my name…and he knew my mom wasn't alive." She pressed trembling hands over her mouth and nose. "Then he asked about a note. Was there a note?"

Alarm bells clanged in his brain. "What did he say, exactly?"

"*Did you get my note?*" she parroted slowly. "That was it. What's he talking about?"

"We'll figure it out. Which direction did he go?"

"There." She pointed. "Toward the meat section in the back."

The store manager, a petite, middle-aged man, joined them, along with two other employees. "Officer, is everything okay?"

"No. There was an incident. Did you call 9-1-1?"

"Yes. They said the police would be here soon."

"Excellent, thank you." Tucker gently guided Sarah toward

the manager and the other two employees. He had to check the back of the store and see where the suspect went. "Sit tight here with them until the officer arrives. I'll be right back."

He jogged toward the store's back door, holding his weapon as he entered the storage and unloading area. Dozens of boxes and crates lined the walls. Two small crates lay on their sides by the receiving doors, along with the crumpled figure of a man.

"Identify yourself." Tucker called out. Disappointment surged as a teenager, maybe seventeen or eighteen with shaggy blond hair and a goatee, rose and held out his hands. He wore a Tops shirt and appeared shell-shocked and confused.

"My name's Joe. I work in receiving." Joe's eyes rounded at the sight of Tucker's gun.

"What happened?" he asked the teen.

"This guy just ran through here, and when I asked what he was doing and said he wasn't allowed to be here, he knocked these produce boxes over and hit me." Blood trickled from the kid's nose as confirmation. "Is that, like, a criminal or something?"

"Yes, something like that."

"Cool, I was part of a crime scene." The kid wore an awed expression.

"Not cool." Tucker shook his head. "We have a missing child in the area and that was likely one of the men who kidnapped him."

"A kid? No way. Like a baby or something?"

"It's a seven-year-old boy. We've had bulletins out since last night."

"Wait, does the boy have, like, reddish-blond hair? Freckles?"

Tucker's spine snapped straight. "He does. Where did you see him?"

"I didn't see him. My buddy Andy and his girlfriend were taking her dog out for a run along the river this morning, and they saw this guy parked near that warehouse place on 62. You know, the big building on the other side of the Allegheny River? Andy said the guy had a kid, and the kid was crying and trying to get away, but the man got him and put him back in the car."

Tucker bit back the obvious question: *Why didn't your friend call the police?* "Do you know what the car looked like?"

"I sure don't, Officer sir, but Andy might."

Tucker snagged his cell from his pocket. *Thank You, Lord.* This could be the break they needed. "What's Andy's full name and number?"

"Andrew Dixon." The young man rattled off his friend's cell phone number, and Tucker typed it into a text to Heath, then briefly mentioned the connection. He sent the text before he addressed the young man. "I'll need your statement too." He examined the backroom. "Did the suspect touch anything?"

"I don't think so. He just kicked those—" he indicated the wood crates labeled *Vegetables* spilled on the ground "—the boxes hit me, and I stumbled back, then he decked me." He wiped the small trickle of nosebleed with his shirt.

"I'm glad you're safe. For now, please let your manager know you have to go to the station to talk to officers about what happened here and what your friend saw. We'll need your full account of today's events as well as help with an artist rendering."

"Okay. Cool." Joe strode past, and Tucker adjusted the grip on his gun, then trod over to the back doors. Most likely the suspect was long gone, but he would at least check for tire marks. The black minivan was at the station getting cleaned for prints. The Camry he'd seen the other night had yet to be located again in the county. There must be at least three suspects involved, maybe four.

He scrutinized the small alleyway outside the receiving area. Paved but strewn with dirt and gravel. A green dumpster sat to the left, and Tucker quietly edged around it. Nothing. He checked inside, but it must've been recently emptied. No signs of the man. About thirty yards away, a small clearing that would work as a makeshift parking spot for smaller vehicles sat empty. He jogged over, careful to avoid the muddied areas on the concrete.

Tucker's mouth flattened. Tire tracks plus several footprints marked the dirt-covered concrete. They could be from employees, or from the man who had just threatened Sarah.

The suspect must've tracked them, following at a distance, then parked here and snuck in through the grocery store's back doors. He must've known they were together, or else the man would've tried to abduct her.

But why? What did Sarah have that they needed? And Liam?

He racked his brain but had no memory of a note.

Tucker blew out a breath, generating a cloud in front of his face as he headed back inside the grocery store. What kind of criminal organization was this that murdered someone in cold blood, then had numerous hit men on hand to take care of another perceived threat—which, unfortunately, was Sarah?

NINE

Sarah sank into the chair in Heath's office as she waited for Heath and Tucker to join her. They had left Mr. Meow at Heath's home, where Tucker had helped her set up the spare bedroom with the litter box, two Tupperware containers for food and water, and a large spare blanket wadded up on the recliner for Mr. Meow to snuggle into. She'd stroked the cat, said goodbye, and shut the door with a heavy heart. At least the sweet feline had a great view of the outdoors through the window and wasn't stuck in a crate anymore. She'd worry about getting his collar on later. He wasn't going anywhere now.

She willed away the tremble that had started at Tops Grocery store and still had a hold of her muscles. The man's voice played through her mind like a broken CD on repeat.

Now, now, Sarah, don't lie. Then: *Did you get my note?*

Had the police officers missed something? He must be one of the men who had her son. She should've begged to go with him. Screamed at him to take her to Liam.

Please, God. Protect Liam and bring him back to me.

Tucker and Heath pushed through the door, Heath settling into his chair behind the desk while Tucker sat beside her. Onyx circled around their chairs then sprawled on his side at her feet. His formidable presence calmed her.

"Someone has a crush," Tucker teased about the dog.

"He likes my longer nails." She flashed her fingers. "Good for scratching." Then she reached down to use them on the dog's thickly furred neck. Onyx sighed happily, and the men chuckled.

They'd been interviewing the teens from the grocery store in another office. "How was the interview?" she asked. "Did you find out anything helpful?"

"Joe's friend Andy gave us more details about what he saw near the river. Andy mentioned a Camry, like the one that took Liam. Andy also said his girlfriend believes one of them had a prominent scar on his cheek."

"That's the man I saw today." Sarah straightened. "It's on his left cheek."

"Okay, good. Andy confirmed that as well. He also said the Camry drove back onto 62 and headed southeast." Heath jotted down a note then looked up. "In addition, we ran the prints from the minivan that chased you last night. The ID came back. Brad Jackson, forty-one. Last residence is in Philadelphia."

"Close to Fountain View," she noted.

"Yes. You're sure the killers never saw you at Tanner's work?" Heath set the pencil down.

"I mean, it's possible. I was crying when I ran out of the lobby, in a hurry to get to Liam."

"I don't think it matters if they saw her," Tucker interjected. "I think they know—knew—Tanner and were aware he was married. Any quick internet search can pull up a picture of Sarah. Especially given her history with swimming and the Olympics."

"Good point," Heath replied. "It's clear they want something from you, Sarah. Now we have a suspect threatening about a note. I've informed all my officers what he said. We'll be on the lookout for a ransom note. In the meantime, we have an APB out for this Brad Jackson. PSP is up to date as well."

Tucker crossed his arms. "I also spoke with Ranger Clay Reiger. He's a new hire, only been here about a year with the forest service, but he's a good guy. Responsible. He notified the rest of the rangers in this county and in the surrounding counties. They'll be on the lookout along the main roads crossing Allegheny National Forest."

"So do you think Liam is still here?" Sarah asked. Just saying his name made her throat tighten and heartrate kick up.

Tucker and Heath exchanged a brooding look that unsettled her, before Tucker answered. "There's no reason to think the men who took him left the area. Andy saw them nearby. Like Heath said, the Pennsylvania State Police are aware and are on the lookout." He gazed at her, his tense expression softening. "I have a call in to Drew Stevens as well. We keep missing each other."

Heath opened his top drawer and tugged out a container of mints, offering one to both of them. She murmured *thanks* and popped it into her mouth. The sharp peppermint flavor bit into her cheek and tongue, reminding her of her son and his universal dislike of peppermint-flavored anything.

"We're getting close, Sarah," Tucker said in a soothing voice. "He'll be in your arms soon."

"Every night I'm away from him feels like I die a little more inside." She crossed her arms and hugged her middle.

"By the way, you're both welcome to stay at my place again tonight." Heath pulled open his drawer and dropped the mints back inside. "We're going to try and decorate the Christmas tree soon, and Piper would love company."

A sense of heaviness permeated the room, and her heart ached for all of them. For Heath, who had lost his wife. For Tucker, losing his brother. And for herself, for her own loss.

She and Tanner hadn't been doing well, but she would never have wanted him snatched from her and Liam's lives like this.

"One more thing." Tucker cleared his throat. "With all that happened today, we forgot to mention the phone call with Alexander Drake."

He was right. The last two days blurred together like Liam's hand running across a rain-splattered window.

"Details?" Heath retrieved his pencil and began writing again.

"Sarah received a call from Alexander Drake earlier," Tucker explained. "He's the CEO of Zeta Pharmaceuticals, where Tanner works. *Worked*," he corrected, his throat bobbing on a swallow. Sarah's heart went out to him. "Mr. Drake was out of the country when Tanner was shot, which may be coincidental, or it may be convenient."

"How well do you know Mr. Drake?" Heath asked her.

"We've met a few times over the last few years. He's a nice enough man, but after all that's happened, I can't say for sure he's not involved. Tanner worked closely with Mark Sousa and with Alexander Drake."

Heath looked up from his scribbling. "Mark Sousa?"

"He's the head scientist behind Nuexta. That's the Parkinson's medication they were working on. Mark oversaw the molecular creation of the project, and he and Tanner worked closely to keep it on a timetable and to report the clinical trial findings so they could move ahead with FDA approval."

"Would you consider Tanner and Mark friends or work acquaintances?"

"They weren't friends. As I told Tucker earlier, they seemed to antagonize each other."

Looking back, she realized there had been an undeniable tension between Tanner, Alexander and Mark the last few months, and it was most likely due to Nuexta.

"Tucker, I hate to bring this up," Heath said quietly, "but you should be aware, if there's something sideways in this medication-creation process, the trials Sarah talked about, and your mom was one of the members of the trial group..."

"She may be subpoenaed as a witness in her son's murder case," Tucker finished, his voice tight as a rope.

"It's imperative we find out what Tanner and these two individuals were at odds about, and tie it to the kidnappers," Heath noted. "I have a feeling that it's putting yours and Liam's lives at risk."

His words sent a gush of ice water down her back.

Heath continued, "Drew Stevens's message said they were securing a warrant to collect Tanner's work laptop and any items in his office at work and at home. In the meantime, we need to recover Tanner's cell phone. You said it's at the cottage?"

She nodded. "In my car. I was so tired when I got here, I didn't unload everything."

"It needs to be secured as evidence in this case." Heath looked expectantly at Tucker. "That may be exactly what the criminals want. I have two officers out on patrol specifically looking for Liam. How about you swing by the cottage. One of my officers is in the area. He can accompany you there."

"That works. I need to stop by Henry Rodgers's too. He's out of town, and I told him I'd keep an eye on his place."

A half an hour later, after dropping Onyx off at Heath's house to rest, Tucker and Sarah drove along Highway 62 toward the cottage. Clouds hung low in the sky, gunmetal gray and ominous. She couldn't help the goosebumps that rose across her limbs as Tucker focused on the road in front and behind them.

"Does Liam take any medications?" he asked.

"Not really. Just for seasonal allergies." She considered the last two years, how difficult they'd been for her little family between the accident, finding out Tanner had been unfaithful and their ensuing marital issues. "Liam started having pretty extreme anxiety and panic attacks recently."

He glanced at her. "That's too bad. Did something happen to spark his anxiety?"

"We were in that car accident a year and a half ago."

"You and Liam?"

"Yes. On my way home from school, someone T-boned us at an intersection near our house. We were okay...but Liam still has nightmares and worries about driving sometimes." They slowed as two deer dashed across the road. "Tanner wanted to try medication for Liam, but I didn't want to take that route. After speaking with his pediatrician and a friend who counsels youth, we—I—decided to get him a cat instead." She snorted softly. "It sounds silly, right? But we're not home enough for a dog, and Mr. Meow came highly recommended."

"Interesting. So, he's a therapy cat?"

"He is. He was trained by a woman who specializes in feline therapy." She blinked out the passenger-side window as an onslaught of emotion battered her. Liam needed the cat as much as Mr. Meow needed him.

"Mr. Meow is safe at Heath's house," Tucker reassured her. "He may not like being shut in that bedroom for the time being, but he has food, water, a soft bed, lots of space to climb and hide. Once we get Liam back, they'll be reunited."

Tucker slowed as they neared Aunt Beverly's cottage. A police car sat in the driveway, and the officer waved when they rolled slowly past. On their left, the Allegheny River glistened silver blue under the fading winter sunlight as they drove the remainder of the way to the Rodgers' cabin.

"I'll be quick at Henry's place."

They parked out front and exited the vehicle together.

Tucker scrutinized the yard and woods out back, his eyes tracing the hedges around the house and the tree line separating the structure from the woods. She crossed her arms and rubbed the opposite arm as chill bumps skittered over her skin.

The Rodgers' place was small and quaint. Family pictures adorned the walls, and a blue couch sat in the living room beside a well-used La-Z-Boy recliner. The kitchen held a round table with four chairs, mahogany cabinets, and child-drawn artwork stuck to the fridge with touristy magnets. The scents of cinnamon and coffee clung to the air, welcoming despite the home's occupants not being present.

Tucker inspected the two bedrooms and checked the windows, the back door and the thermometer, then he peered out from the curtained kitchen window. He let out a thoughtful noise.

Sarah came up next to him. "What is it?"

"Henry's workshop door isn't shut all the way. I'm pretty sure that was closed when I left last time." He released the curtain fabric and settled on his heels, tapping out a quick text. "I'll let Officer Venetta know." A few moments later, he slid his cell back in his pocket. "He said he'd come over."

After one more sweep of the Rodgers' place, the crunch of tires on gravel announced Officer Venetta's arrival. They exited the house to join him in the driveway. Daylight was running out, and this area offered no streetlights and few house lights to brighten the dark stretch of road.

Sarah's heart thumped wildly against her ribs. Would she ever feel safe here again?

Tucker checked in with Officer Venetta, then turned to Sarah. "He's on a call with Heath, and he'll wait out here."

Tucker headed toward the large workshop. "Let's get this done so we can get out of here."

She sidled up beside him as they approached the building, Tucker gripping his weapon. Her heart climbed into her throat.

"Have the police been at my aunt Beverly's cottage since..." She gulped. "Since Liam was taken?"

"They were there through the first night, but I'm not certain they stayed after that. Heath posted an officer there this morning because of the phone, but I don't know about the overlap. They were going to break into the vehicle to get it, but figured we'd wait for you to unlock it so your car isn't damaged."

He stepped inside the workshop first. Sarah followed, glancing backward periodically. No one would come after them with Officer Venetta right there. Still, her heart wouldn't settle.

"Hold up." Tucker froze, and she bumped into him.

She squinted into the well-lit room. A dark gray sedan parked in the space, and two sawhorses lay on their side, chunks of wood strewn about the floor like the car had struck them while it was backed in.

"Is that the—"

"Yes." He hissed out an exhale. "The car the men who kidnapped Liam were driving." He motioned for her to stay near the door. "Looks like someone used this as a hiding spot. They must've figured out the Rodgers aren't home, waited until the police had left your aunt's cottage and brought this here to ditch it."

Tucker circled the vehicle, then let out a surprised cry. "Whoa." He whipped out his cell and hit a button.

"What is it?" A violent tremble stole over her limbs.

"Stay back." His voice was unnaturally strident, and she cowered from its intensity and the look on his face as he turned around and spoke into his phone. "Venetta. We need you in here. Let Heath know I'm going to need a forensics team. Call the ME too." He briefly met Sarah's eyes, and the hard-packed emotion she saw there felt like a slap to the face.

He hung up and rammed a hand through his hair.

"What's an ME?" she asked.

"Medical examiner. It's not Liam, but there's a body in the car."

Tucker's muscles shook as Officer Venetta joined them in the workshop, his jangling utility belt the only sound amidst dead silence. In the distance, a siren wailed. Praise the Lord, the body was an adult man. Not a child.

Not Liam.

"Looks like two gunshot wounds to the chest," Officer Venetta noted, taking pictures. "Make that three." The seasoned officer had been part of the Holloway police force for at least three decades, and Tucker had known both Anthony and his wife, Eleanor, for most of his life. Tucker didn't miss the way Anthony's hands trembled as he clicked pictures.

"It's not Liam," Sarah repeated softly, over and over to herself. "It's not Liam."

"Looks like the victim has a big gash on his arm." Venetta whistled. "Could this be—"

"That's the guy who ran us off the road and stabbed a hole in my Bronco's back window." Tucker grimaced at the bloody wound. "The other men must've turned on him when he wanted to get medical attention."

Tucker finished helping Officer Venetta, then went over to Sarah. She was shivering, her cheeks damp, a wild look clouding her eyes, and she lunged into his arms. For a heartbeat or two, he relished her embrace, losing his train of thought about this crime and the *whys* plaguing him.

"It's okay, I'm here," he spoke into her soft hair. "He's alive. I promise." *Lord, let it be true. Help us find him, please.*

She nodded vigorously, then backed up as though she realized they weren't alone. Another officer burst into the workshop, followed by an older, balding man in slacks and a polo shirt and carrying a leather briefcase.

Officer Venetta motioned to the two new people. "This is Officer Gregg, and this here's Martin Drummond, the county medical examiner. He lives on the other side of Simmons Hill, just a few minutes away." Venetta threw a thumb at Tucker and Sarah. "This is Tucker Brindley, a ranger with the US Forest Service. And Sarah Brindley. Tucker found the deceased while checking the Rodgers' place."

Tucker nodded hello.

"Good evening to you both. I am not pleased that this is happening near my house," Martin remarked sourly as he slipped on blue nitrile gloves and made his way toward the vehicle, his small, dark eyes intent on the scene. "This is the position in which you found the body?"

"Yes. We haven't touched anything." Tucker shielded Sarah from the line of sight of the man slumped forward in the front seat. Three tiny holes in the glass showed what had happened. The dead man must've parked the car, then his partner ambushed him.

Heath slipped through the door, a grim expression wreathing his face. "Any idea who the deceased is?"

"Not officially, until they take the body to the morgue and we check for ID. But I have a thought…" Tucker let his sentence run off, his gaze bouncing from Heath to Sarah and back. Sarah had her cell out, swiping through the screen.

He edged over to Heath. "I have a feeling it's Brad Jackson, the man who was driving the minivan. We've got his prints, and whoever is running this show must know he's been ID'd. Useless to them. A liability, actually."

"Right." Heath shifted his feet.

"But how did they get this here without being recognized?" Tucker pondered aloud.

"We had officers at the cottage for most of the last twenty-four hours. There may have been a two- or three-hour window where they could use Old Forge Road from Geneva Township. Under cover of night, it's possible." Heath scratched his neck. "Once we get the deceased's prints, we'll—"

"Tucker!" Sarah rushed over. "I just got a text from an unknown number. You need to see this."

Tucker grabbed her cell, and his stomach pitched into his shoes.

A trade. The mother for the son. Or else she'll end up just like him.

"No. Absolutely not." Did the kidnappers mean *him*, as in, Liam? Or *him*, as in the deceased man in the car? Tucker scrubbed a hand down his face.

Neither option was acceptable.

"Venetta." Heath leaned over Tucker's shoulder. "We need a trace." He turned to Tucker. "Let's get Tanner's cell phone now, then head back to the station."

They drove to her aunt's cottage, parked in the driveway, and he and Heath got out. Sarah climbed out slowly after them, keeping close to Tucker.

"I'd like to look inside first," Heath noted. "You have a code for this, correct?"

"I do." She stared warily at the front yard for a moment, then they bookended her to the front door, where she punched in a code. "It's 1-0-1-1."

When they entered the cottage, Tucker and Heath gripped their weapons and listened carefully. No cars around the building meant anyone nearby would have to have come a long distance on foot. Unlikely this time of year.

"Anything look out of place?" Tucker asked.

"Everything looks just like when we—when I was here last," she answered, her posture wilting.

Tucker winced. Poor Sarah. Everything must remind her of Liam. Of the fact that he'd been taken.

They finished up inside, then returned to the front porch. Heath and Tucker rechecked the area before Sarah led them to the garage out back. She hung close to Tucker, her fingers brushing his wrist as they approached the structure.

Heath went in first, gun drawn, then he called Tucker inside. Tucker guided Sarah in ahead of him.

"This is your vehicle?" Tucker asked.

"It is. There's a keypad on the side, which I use to get in."

Tucker addressed Heath. "Let's check the engine to make sure no one messed with it."

"Good idea."

Tucker and Heath combed through the exterior of the vehicle and the undercarriage, looking for any marks or dents or obvious signs of foul play. It appeared to be a new model, and the keypad along the driver-side door seemed untouched.

Still, his gut warned him to be cautious.

"I don't see anything unusual." Heath said to Tucker, then addressed Sarah. "Did you leave it locked?"

"I honestly don't remember. Yesterday was a blur."

"It's alright." Tucker reached over and patted her arm, then motioned at Heath. "I'd like to see inside before we open the doors."

Heath made a frustrated sound. "I need to grab my flashlight. Be right back." He jogged out of the garage.

Tucker moved around the car toward Sarah. He didn't like being too far from her, especially given what they just found in Henry Rodgers' garage. Keeping her close meant he could keep her safe. *That's the only reason.*

"This is a fancy ride," he teased.

"Tanner bought it after our accident." A frown marred her lovely features. "I miss my old Tahoe, but it was totaled."

He shot her a sympathetic look.

"I could use my phone light." Sarah thumbed the bright light on her cell and flashed it at the back of her vehicle. "It's just the way I left it, what—" She gasped, her mouth going slack. "Liam's shoes! And his pajamas from the other night. What are they doing here?"

"Show me where they are."

"There?" She pointed, and Tucker leaned in. A pair of Crocs sat on the back seat atop a wrinkled pile of boy's pjs. "How did those get in my car?" She reached up under the spot above the license plate. "What if they—"

"Sarah, don't!"

Too late. She touched the button to open the trunk. A flash of light blinded him as a blast of heat exploded before them. They were thrown backward, into the garage wall, and Tucker gasped as the air was slapped out of his lungs. He fought through the feeling of temporary paralysis and scrambled across the ground to cover her with his body as metal and plastic rained down.

The criminals must've wired an explosive device to go off when the vehicle's trunk was opened. No doubt they intended to hurt or kill when officers went for Tanner's phone. He forced in a breath as he felt along her arm to her neck. Black spots dotted his eyesight, and his good ear rang from the noise.

"Sarah, are you okay?" Nothing. He lifted her into his arms as the smoke and debris cleared. Tucker struggled to his feet, Sarah held to his chest as Heath burst through the garage door.

But his eyes were on Sarah. Blood matted her hair, and her head lolled back.

Was she unconscious…or worse?

TEN

Sarah awoke to the sound of wheels and whipping material, like a sheet, coupled with the cloying scent of industrial-grade cleaners and latex gloves. Her world shook and trembled like an earthquake. What— Where was she?

Her head felt soggy, her brain stuck in a sleep she couldn't quite pull herself out of. A throbbing ache came from her temples, and when she opened her eyes, all she could make out was white, bright lights. The garage at the cottage.

Where was—

"Tucker?" Sandpaper lined her throat. When she licked her lips, the metallic flavor of blood tinged her tongue, and she recoiled. "Tucker?" she tried again, louder, then tried moving her arms and legs.

"Ma'am, please hold still. We're going to get you into a room."

Who was that?

"Hey, I'm here." A large presence filled her peripheral vision. *Tucker.* "We're at the hospital. You're on a stretcher, just got a couple bumps and bruises."

She drew in a large gulp of Lysol-scented air. "Hospital?" *Liam.* The shoes and clothes she'd seen in her car. "Liam?"

There was a long enough pause that even in her incapacitated state she knew the answer. Tears gathered at the corners of her eyes, spilling down to her ears.

They hadn't found him yet.

The nurse slowed, mouthing something to Tucker over Sarah's head. They entered a room, then the nurse and another set of arms helped her onto a lumpy metal bed. Everything spun.

Finally, the nurse exited the room, leaving Sarah with Tucker looming over her. Had he helped pick her up?

"Do you need anything?" The attentive way he asked brought more tears.

"My throat... Water please?" She fumbled for the water glass beside the bed. He grasped it and guided it to her lips, and she drank a long drag of the cool liquid. After she was done, he set the cup down and gently wiped the stray tears from her cheek and jawline.

"What happened at my aunt's cottage? In the garage?"

"Do you remember opening the back of your car?"

"I saw... Liam's shoes, right?"

"Yes." He picked a piece of lint or dirt from his shirt, then met her eyes. "The men who killed Brad Jackson—he was ID'd a few minutes ago—we think they rigged your vehicle so when it was opened, a small explosive device in the trunk went off. The doctor thinks you hit your head on the metal tool rack when we were thrown back. Thank the Lord it wasn't worse."

She reached up, feeling the bandage spanning her forehead. Pain radiated under her fingertips, but they must've given her medication, because her head felt faraway, like she was detached from her body.

Tucker collapsed into the chair beside the bed, his elbows on his knees and his face grim. "I'm so grateful you're okay. I thought..." His words trailed off, and Sarah's heart did a funny skip-hop like when Liam climbed to the highest point on the park swing set and pretended he was going to jump off.

"Liam needs his mom," he whispered.

"I miss him." Her throat burned. "So much. I just want him safe in my arms again."

He covered one of her hands with his. "We're going to find him."

She continued in a broken voice. "The text...it said they want me instead of him. I'll do it. I *want* them to take me instead. Please, Tucker."

"Let's pray it doesn't come to that." He shook his head. "We're doing everything we can to find him. You are strong, Sarah. I need you to hang on to hope. Hang on for Liam." He swiped at his cheek, and she was mesmerized at the shimmering she saw there. Tanner had never cried in front of her. Ever.

He squared his shoulders before continuing. "We *will* get him back. But please, we can't lose you in the process."

"If I don't get my son back, I'm already lost."

"Sarah." Her name was an admonition. "You're never lost. God sees you, every part of you. He loves you and Liam."

She closed her eyes as her secret shame returned, a hidden wound buried in the depths of her soul. "Liam was going to be a big brother."

Tucker drew back in surprise. "I didn't know that."

"No one did. Just me and Tanner."

"You suffered a miscarriage?"

Guilt poked and prodded her, uncovering her remorse and daring her to share it. Daring her to contradict him. As Tucker's clear blue gaze held her steady, free of condemnation, the dam of her regrets and emotions broke.

"No." She covered her face with her hands, the bandage chaffing her fingertips like her mistake chaffed her heart. "I was...scared. Tanner and I were at odds all the time." She dropped her hands as the pain of Tanner's indiscretion returned. "He was working a lot, and I was angry that he never put his son first. That he never put me first. After I had Liam, I struggled for months to keep my head above water. I had pretty bad postpartum issues."

"I didn't realize that, and I'm sorry things were so difficult, Sarah. You also didn't have a mom to come alongside you. That must've made things even worse."

His understanding broke down the rest of her defenses, and the painful truth spilled out. "I ended the pregnancy, Tucker. I hate saying it out loud. It was early on, but I ended it because I was scared. Of all of it. Of being a single mom like my mom had been. Of Tanner's coldness. Of feeling sad and alone again. So alone." She smothered her sobs with her palms.

Tucker reached over, clasping her hands, his fingers threading with hers. Anchoring her. "I'm here," he whispered.

"I think of that baby every day. And I can't help but believe Liam's kidnapping is the result of what I did to that poor little…" Her keening cry came from the depths of her soul.

Suddenly, the bed sank down and two strong arms came around her. She wasn't alone anymore. Tucker sat beside her, holding her so close she wasn't sure where she started and he ended. He cradled her gently as she cried and told him about the baby she never met.

"In my heart I know it was another little boy. They would've been brothers. Friends. Playmates. Teammates." Tucker handed her a tissue. She wiped her nose, her face. "I stole Liam's chance at having a little brother because I was just like her."

"Your mom?"

"Yes. She got pregnant twice with that…that man's child. And twice, she borrowed money from him and came back… without the baby." She crumpled up the tissue and tossed it to the bedside table. "And I'm no better than her. I tried to be, but I did the same thing."

A nurse appeared in the doorway and cleared her throat as

she entered. They both looked up, and Sarah startled, trying to get away from Tucker. He held her fast.

"Ms. Brindley needs a moment. Would you mind coming back in a few minutes, please?" he asked calmly, and the nurse nodded once, then turned and left.

"Sarah, you are nothing like your mom. Granted, I never met her, but from what you told me and Tanner, she was a mess. You're an amazing person. Strong. Caring. A loving mom. Olympic swimmer. Tanner mentioned how good you were with Liam when he was a baby. How patient you were with him. Listen, you could've given up after all you'd been through, but you didn't. You're a fighter, and I'm so proud of you."

She shook her head, unsure how to accept his praise.

"Heath was right. When I found out the day you were swimming your event, I gathered a watch party with some of our friends and the youth group." He ducked his chin, and his sudden shyness brought another lump to Sarah's throat. "You got on that starting block, and I was blown away by you. I *knew* you, the real you, and knew what you'd overcome. How I wish I'd been on the pool deck to give you a hug when you finished. Win or lose."

"You really did all that, just for me?"

He held out his palms playfully. "Busted."

Was he saying all this to make her feel better? She folded inward, hearing what he said but still filled with agony over her past mistakes. Unworthiness had become such a close comrade she didn't know how to separate herself from it.

"Now, don't shut me out. I'm not done. You're running a swim-lesson business and coaching a swim team, all while being a wife and mother. Don't sell yourself short or minimize how far you've come." He paused, a faraway look in his eyes. "Do you remember the time we went on that youth retreat to

Hersheypark? We were too old, but Tanner begged for us to go as chaperones?"

Memories flashed back. The three-hour bus ride there, seated beside chatty and outgoing Tanner but wishing she'd been able to sit beside Tucker, who was quietly talking to two girls considered outsiders in the youth group. By then—four weeks into her six-week training in Erie—Sarah was taken by the Brindley twins. By Tanner's effervescent and welcoming personality and by Tucker's kind steadiness and hidden depths of humor.

During their time at Hersheypark, Tanner had been glued to her side. But after one of the other youth leaders had gotten sick and the youth pastor asked Tanner to take the young man to the medical area to rest and rehydrate, Tucker had quietly stepped in and offered to ride the rest of the rides with Sarah and her quartet of giggling high school girls.

Tucker's thoughtful actions and teasing comments had put her at ease as the six of them roamed the park, and she'd found herself wondering why he'd never shown interest in her like Tanner had. Found herself wondering what it would be like to hold Tucker Brindley's hand, not Tanner's.

Then Tanner had returned and promptly inserted himself back into their group, and Tucker's kind but aloof demeanor resumed.

"Yes, I remember that trip. You made me go on the SooperDooperLooper, and I almost died." She elbowed him lightly in the ribs. "Anyway, what about it?"

"When Pastor Tom talked about Jesus on the bus ride home, did you…understand what he was saying?"

She tucked in her chin. On a logical level, she knew who Jesus was. Knew He was God's son. Her mom had taken her to church a few times through her childhood, mostly in between boyfriends. But God had always felt like a vague, faraway father figure rather than a close, loving friend, the way Pastor Tom had identified Jesus.

"Pastor Tom shared the Gospel," Tucker continued. "God's finished work on the cross through His son, Jesus. The Bible says your sins are washed white as snow, Sarah. You know how when it snows, all the browns and dead colors of fall and winter disappear under the bright whiteness?"

She lifted a shoulder, unsure how to acknowledge that she heard what he said but was fairly certain that verse was meant for others. Not for her.

Was it?

"That applies to you, too, Sarah," he whispered near her ear. "Don't dirty up what God asked Jesus to wipe clean. Don't throw away His grace."

Heath poked his head into the room, eyes widening. "How's it going?" he asked cautiously.

"Well," Tucker answered lightly, extricating himself from her to stand and stretch. "The patient is currently undergoing a stern talking-to by yours truly."

"And what would that be about?" Heath stepped inside.

Tucker gazed at her, and she couldn't help but recognize that he saw her, all of who she was, and he wasn't repulsed by it. Wasn't upset with her.

"We were discussing God's grace. What's up? Any news on Brad's time of death?"

"Haven't heard from the ME yet. We swept the Camry for prints, and I'm waiting on those as well. Next, we need to identify what vehicle they're currently using."

"Clearly, we're dealing with a criminal organization with no lack of funds," Tucker said. "Have local and state authorities been updated about what we found at the Rodgers' place?"

"Yes. PSP are on it, and they've been checking vehicles throughout Allegheny National Forest."

"What about the New York State line? Jamestown?"

"Already on it. I let the N-Y State Police know, as well as Eli's office. The FBI will likely be getting involved." Heath drummed his fingers on his phone for several moments. "Also, I have a few questions for Sarah." When he met her eyes, her breath caught. Why was Heath looking at her that way?

"Okay," she said cautiously, still feeling weak from the explosion and from baring her heart to Tucker.

Tucker motioned at the chair. Heath stepped over, choosing to remain standing, hands resting on his utility belt.

"I finally spoke to Drew Stevens. Nice guy, by the way. Alexander Drake was interviewed, and he's still considered a person of interest despite no current evidence tying him to Tanner's murder."

She swallowed, glancing up at Tucker as he paced around the bed. It was difficult to believe Mr. Drake could be behind Tanner's death, but at this point, little would surprise her.

"They must've gotten Tanner's cell before us," Heath said quietly. "It was cleared of all data."

"What?" Her chest deflated. "Then why did they leave it in my car?"

"We think they were targeting police officers, not you. They didn't necessarily expect you to be there. We're working to locate the local internet service provider and approach them with a warrant to obtain the call records."

She frowned. "How did they get my number to text me?"

"Finding your number would've been easy. They had Tanner's contacts," Tucker noted. "They probably hacked in."

"There's one other thing I found." Heath reached back to rub his neck, his gaze jumpy.

Her pulse pounded in her temples. "Did you find out information about Liam?"

"We've had no updates about Liam, I'm afraid. But Tanner's cell…the only item still on the phone is a picture."

Sarah tilted her head. "Picture of what?"

"Of you and Mark Sousa."

Tucker studied Sarah's face as Heath revealed the picture on Tanner's cell. The criminals were likely trying to incriminate her. Still, Tucker's breath got knocked clear out of him when he saw the image of Sarah with her hair swept up, tendrils framing her beautiful face. She wore a long turquoise gown that fit her slender but strong frame like a glove and sparkling high-heeled shoes peeking out from beneath it.

She stood hip to hip with a person he assumed was Mark Sousa, a handsome, dark-haired man with thick brows and a flat gaze. Even in the picture, arrogance rolled off the man, and seeing his hand riding her lower back made heat rush to Tucker's face.

Was there a connection between Sarah and Mark Sousa? Had something—

No. He didn't believe it. Sarah wasn't her mom. She was a woman of character, who cared deeply about her son and from all accounts had been faithful to Tanner. He wouldn't entertain any other ideas.

Sarah sat up in the bed, her chest rising and falling faster. "Wait. The men who kidnapped Liam are trying to link me and Mark Sousa?"

"It appears that way. They're wrong, though, aren't they?" Heath asked calmly. Too calmly.

"Yes," she replied immediately.

"If there's anything more you need to—"

"Heath," Tucker growled, coming to stand beside Sarah. "Take it easy."

Sarah swallowed. "Those pictures were taken at the grand

opening of the new lab at Zeta Pharmaceuticals. It was more than a year ago. Mr. Drake had a ribbon-cutting ceremony, and Tanner wanted me to attend. I promise you the smile you see there is manufactured."

"But you did know Mark Sousa?" Heath asked casually, eyeballing Tucker. "I mean, you had met him."

"Once or twice. I wanted nothing to do with him. He's well-known for...well, let's just say he's been married at least three times and has quite a reputation at the company as a womanizer."

"And he went after you?" Heath asked.

Sarah shot a wounded glare at him, then Tucker laid a hand on her shoulder. "All right, Heath, that's it for today."

"It's okay." She cleared her throat. "I have nothing to hide. Yes, Mark Sousa came on to me. But that's nothing unusual. From what I've heard, he hits on any living, breathing female in a twenty-foot radius. I'm nothing special."

"Sure, you are," Tucker said before he'd given his words much introspection. "No doubt you were the most beautiful woman there that night." He gnawed his cheek. Why had he said that aloud?

Sarah stared at Tucker as Heath wagged his head back and forth before continuing. "You took the obligatory pictures with the head scientist, who also happened to be a womanizer. Who also happens to have disappeared after Tanner's death and is the main suspect."

"I haven't lived a perfect life, but I'm not a murderer." A cloud passed over her features, and she pressed her curled fingers to her brows.

"That's enough for now," Tucker warned.

"Okey doke." Heath took the hint and headed for the door, but turned and addressed Sarah one more time. "I do need to see you at the station when you're ready. For what it's worth,

Tuck, I know she's not responsible for Tanner's death. But I have to take due course in this investigation and make sure all avenues are checked and rechecked. You understand, right?"

"I understand she's had a rough day and needs to rest." Tucker jabbed his thumb at the hallway, and Heath shook his head, then took his leave.

"Thank you."

"For what?" Tucker asked. "Keeping Heath from being a jerk today?"

"He's not being a jerk. I understand why he's asking. I just can't believe those horrible men would do that. Take my son *and* make it look like I'm part of this. I would never..."

Her features crumpled, and he leaned down so they were eye to eye.

"You're not your mother, Sarah." He gently framed her face with his palms. "Remember what I said. Once you ask for God's forgiveness, your sins are wiped away. You're white as snow. Forgiven."

"Thank you for not hating me."

"I couldn't hate you. Ever." In fact, he was too close to the opposite. *Loving her.*

"I've never spoken to anyone else about that loss. Amy—Drew's wife—struggled with infertility, and I thought telling her would damage our friendship. Tanner was upset—he shut me out. When we were younger, and you and I had chances to talk, you always felt like someone I could trust. Like a best friend."

Tucker averted his gaze so she wouldn't see the hurt in his eyes.

Best friend.

While he'd once longed to be that for her, it was just a small part of the relationship he'd hoped for. Most of all, he'd wanted her heart. Her whole heart.

But Liam was still missing, and that had to be his focus. Plus Sarah had never expressed any interest in him other than as just that—a friend.

ELEVEN

Sarah and Tucker arrived at Heath's house the next morning after another night without any news of Liam's whereabouts. She winced as an ache expanded through her chest. *Please, God, bring him back to me.*

She'd stayed overnight at the hospital to remain under doctor observation, with the promise from Heath that Piper would take care of Mr. Meow. The nurse had given her a pain reliever, and she'd slept heavily for part of the night after that. Around 3:00 a.m. she'd jarred awake at the sight of Tucker sprawled in the chair beside her. It had been startling—and reassuring.

Tucker, that stubborn, sweet man, had spent the night in her hospital room, a makeshift guard and a comfort in the cold sterility of the hospital.

When she'd first met the Brindley boys, Tanner and his attention had made her feel alive. But Tucker had made her feel protected. Cherished. She'd chosen the former, and now she realized how important it was to have someone in her life who had her back. Who would be there for her no matter what.

"You're sure you don't need to go to the ranger station and work?" she asked as they made their way up the sidewalk.

"My supervisor said I could take a few days off to help with the case." He stretched his arms then twisted side to side. "Right now, I just want to see my boy."

So do I, though she knew he meant Onyx. "And get some sleep."

"I'll sleep when Liam is safe in your arms."

Her eyes stung at his matter-of-fact, determined words.

They stepped up on the front porch, and Tucker entered a code. A chorus of barking exploded behind the door like popcorn kernels in a microwave. Piper was at school, and the house was quiet. The officer who had followed them home waved, then drove off, and she was reminded again of her precarious situation. Reminded of the text she'd received yesterday.

A trade. The mother for the son. Or else she'll end up just like him.

Her breath hitched.

As soon as they walked in, Onyx butted his muzzle into Tucker's leg, then turned his long sleek body for back scratches while the other two dogs swarmed her.

"You miss me, boy?" Tucker squatted down, Onyx's tongue lapping at his cheek. He laughed and turned his face away, wiping the slobber from his jaw.

They stood up, and a gleam of moisture on Tucker's neck caught her eye.

Dog slobber. "Let me get that." She located a tissue box on the bar between the kitchen and living room, and swiped a tissue. Stepping so close she could make out his thick, dark eyelashes, she wiped off the remaining dog slobber from Tucker's neck. His smell—cedar and fresh air—filled her nose, and she noticed his chest rise and fall unsteadily.

She dared to look up and found herself caught in his gaze like a fish in a net. Familiar warmth emanated from his eyes, and something else. Admiration? Affection? Their connection felt like an electrical current, and Sarah stepped back, crumpling the tissue and striding over to the black trash can below the counter to toss it.

"Onyx drool is the gift that keeps on giving." Tucker joked. "It's hard to say no when he wants to give kisses."

"A small price to pay for his unwavering devotion." She paused, her words softening. "He adores you."

Tucker glanced sideways at her, wearing an odd expression. Once again, she felt magnetized by the sense that something inside of him could heal what was broken inside of her.

Sarah, stop. He hadn't shown any interest in her back then, and the only interest he showed now came from his concern about Liam. His nephew.

"Heath said there are drinks in the fridge. Pop, iced tea. Juice. Water."

"Thanks." She opened the fridge, located an iced tea and opened it. The liquid cooled her throat. "I should check on Mr. Meow." She capped the drink, set it on the counter, and trotted toward the stairwell. "He'll want to see a familiar face."

"Hey, wait."

She turned. "What's up?"

He held out a circular object. "Here's Mr. Meow's collar, if you want to put that on. It was in the bag with Onyx's medication."

"Good idea." She took it from him, then sucked in a breath. *What was that?*

A small white piece of paper poked out from the large ID tag on Mr. Meow's collar. When they'd gotten Mr. Meow, Liam had chosen an oversize ID tag with a spot to tuck in a picture of the animal, sort of like a locket but slightly larger, to go on his collar.

"Tucker, look. Something is sticking out of the ID locket part!"

"Hold up. Don't touch it." He spun around, flinging open drawers and cabinets. Finally, he grabbed a box of gloves from a small drawer beside the sink. He slipped the gloves on then lifted the collar from her fingers and carefully turned it around so they could peer at the piece of paper in the locket ID.

"I'm going to pull it out."

He pinched his gloved pointer finger and thumb over the tiny piece of paper and tugged. It stuck fast. "They jammed it in here pretty good."

They. He must mean the men who kidnapped Liam. She shivered, part anticipation, part fear. He gave it another tug, and the paper dislodged. He caught it in his palm, then brought it closer to inspect.

Tucker set the collar on one of the kitchen chairs then carefully unfolded the tiny note. A ripped-off piece of paper, jagged around the edges like her soul with Liam gone.

"They put it in the collar knowing we'd see it when we found Mr. Meow." She clenched her hands. "This is what the man at the grocery store meant."

"I'm sure it is." He squinted down at the wrinkled paper.

"What does it say?"

After several moments, he looked away from the note, his jaw ticking. "It doesn't matter. They're playing a game."

"And my son's life is on the line! Please, Tucker. I need to know."

He exhaled harshly. "It says, *Your life for his.*"

Her heart somersaulted. "Is that it? Did they say anything else?"

"No." His throat bobbed on a swallow.

She sank onto a kitchen chair, her ears buzzing with the sound of a hundred bees.

Tucker set the items on a piece of paper towel on the counter, then called Heath. He relayed what they had found, then hung up and turned to her.

Her head suddenly felt like it weighed a hundred pounds, and she let it drop to the kitchen table. "What do you think this means?"

"I'm not sure," Tucker hedged, and she sensed he was holding back.

"Don't hide things from me. I need my son back."

"There's nothing I want more either." He swallowed. "They want you, and they won't give up—or give Liam back—until they have you. There must be something...a specific reason they need you."

She lifted her head and looked him dead in the eye. "And *you* need bait to find out what."

"Yes," he ground out.

"Okay then, let's do this." Her mouth was cotton, her tongue sticking to the roof of her mouth. "Use me as bait."

"Absolutely not. You are not using my friend as bait."

Tucker grimaced as Amy Stevens's voice crackled over the speakerphone. Sarah was hanging out with Piper in the station break room while he, Heath and Officer Drew Stevens—a ten-year-deputy with the Fountain View PD—discussed the case in Heath's office. Officer Stevens was off work today, but he'd agreed to speak about the case if they didn't mind Amy listening.

"I don't want Sarah involved in this at all," she reiterated.

"She's already involved, ma'am," Tucker answered. "We would protect her. Be at her back. She wouldn't be alone."

"What about the suspect who underwent surgery yesterday?" Officer Stevens asked.

"One of my men was just there," Heath replied. "He's still recovering from surgery, and the first thing out of his mouth when we questioned him was pleading the fifth. He wants a lawyer, of course. It'll be days before we can interview him. Liam doesn't have days. Mrs. Stevens, I know it sounds bad—"

"Bad?" Amy interrupted. "Do you have any idea what Sarah has been through already?"

"We do not," Tucker noted respectfully. What had Tanner done to her? "Care to enlighten us?"

"Is this Tucker Brindley?"

"Yes, ma'am, it is."

"Tanner—your brother—basically let Sarah raise Liam alone. He traveled all the time while in sales at Zeta, then when he was working on that stupid medication he was gone a lot too. He also left her to take care of his ailing mom. Sarah had to cut back on her swim lessons because Tanner wasn't home. He was too busy—" Amy stopped short.

"He was too busy doing what?" Heath prompted.

"I don't want to disrespect my dear friend or your family, Tucker, because Sarah thinks highly of you and she loves your mom. But your *brother*," she spit out the word, "was cheating on her. He'd been seeing his secretary, and when Sarah found out, that snake didn't bother denying it."

The urge to punch the wall while imagining it was his twin's face almost overtook Tucker's good sense. Tanner was gone. What good would that do? What a fool his brother had been. Sarah's words returned to him. Her heavy-hearted reveal about her decision to end her pregnancy last year. Her pain and grief. Was it also because she'd known about the cheating?

"Did Sarah know about his infidelity?" he asked.

"Yes. It was the hardest decision I've made, telling my best friend and one of the most caring people I know that I saw her husband leaving a fancy restaurant in Philadelphia with a leggy brunette on a night Sarah thought he was supposed to be in Baltimore. The day Tanner died, she was going to warn him about the clinical trials and your mom, but she was also going to tell him he had to change or else she was leaving him."

Sarah had been thinking about leaving Tanner?

Heath rifled through the paperwork on his desk. "Let's move on so we don't take any more of your time. Drew, you said you've cleared Alexander Drake as a suspect? Is that correct?"

"We're keeping an eye on him, but as of now, yes. He wasn't in the country, and as far as we've seen in the evidence we collected, there's no connection between the men who killed Tanner and Drake."

"Right. What about the security cameras?"

"The system was up and running, but the cameras on the third floor weren't working," Drew Stevens replied wearily. "It had shorted out the night before Tanner was murdered. We think they were planning on ambushing him there and made sure there would be no evidence."

"Guys, I hate to break up this party, but my husband just worked three twelves in a row. Drew really needs to sleep." Amy hesitated. "Tucker, if you're as wonderful as Sarah always said, please take care of her. Find Liam. And don't use her as bait to catch these killers."

They hung up, and he and Heath faced each other across the desk.

"Wonderful, huh?" Heath said it straight-faced, but Tucker knew he was being ribbed.

"Shut it," he growled. "We can't use her as bait until we find out where the men are, anyway." He rammed a hand through his hair. "I can't stand the thought of her getting hurt. Or worse. I just want to save her son."

"For Sarah or for Liam?" Heath asked.

"Both. They need each other." And *he* needed *her*, but that was irrelevant. She'd made her choice, and though he'd tried to wipe them from memory, her comments to Tanner about his hearing loss still stung.

"She must be blind, man." Heath chuckled, the sound grating on Tucker like sandpaper on wood.

"You say that because...?"

"You love her. It's written on your face, it's always been there."

"She made her choice years ago," Tucker snapped back. "She didn't want me."

"How could she make a choice without knowing there *was* a choice to make?"

"I am too tired to figure out riddles. I was there that summer. She could've...we could've...but we didn't."

"Tanner made sure that was the case."

"He didn't want to share her, and I don't blame him. When you have a woman like Sarah Baxter—like Sarah *Brindley*—you hold on tight and don't let go."

Heath's cell buzzed, and he tapped the screen, putting in on speaker. "Calhoun here."

"Hey, boss, Venetta was tipped off about some bloody clothes behind a bakery in town. A jacket and a shirt. Some teenagers were back there earlier and saw it."

Tucker straightened, eyes crashing into Heath's as they listened.

"Got it. Meet me there in twenty minutes." Heath ended the call, and he and Tucker stood. A lead.

Thank You, Lord.

It felt like a hundred extra pounds had lifted off his shoulders. Heath came around the desk and swatted Tucker's arm. "Amy is right."

Tucker narrowed his eyes. "About what?"

"You *are* wonderful."

Tucker punched his friend's bicep, then turned and headed to the break room to check on Sarah and tell her about the clothing they'd just found out about.

She was the one who was wonderful, and she didn't deserve what was happening to her. Didn't deserve for her son and herself to be targeted by these killers.

And his love for her had nothing to do with it.

TWELVE

Sarah took in the sad string of Christmas lights strung across the bakery, sagging in the middle like her heart in her chest. How could she even think about celebrating this season with Liam gone?

As they waited in the police vehicles for the officers to locate the bloody clothes they'd been tipped off about, a memory floated through her mind. Christmas service when she was a child. Mom had kicked out Eddy, her latest dirtbag boyfriend, and she had brought eight-year-old Sarah to a candlelight service. Sarah had been mesmerized by the small church sanctuary as the pastor led them in acapella hymns about calm, silent nights, angels singing on high and a manger among the livestock that held baby Jesus.

Sarah had cradled her candle carefully, transfixed by the flickering little light, careful not to let the dripping wax through the star-shaped paper around the bottom of the candle stick. When she'd looked at her mom, there'd been glimpses of peace on her world-weary features. Sarah had frozen that moment in time, those emotions, those words in the songs that somehow promised joy and hope when her life didn't hold much of either.

"Hey, you should probably head over to Eli's car." Tucker turned, and their eyes caught and clung like tinsel on a Christmas tree. She noted the hard contours of his cheeks, the grizzled beard on his jaw and the way the sunlight reflected in his blue eyes.

A knock on the driver-side door jolted them both. Heath stood outside, and Tucker rolled the window down. "You ready?"

"Sure." She frowned at the second police officer sitting in his unmarked car across the lot. Tucker and Heath wanted her to wait with him while they investigated the area. She stepped out, and Heath motioned her toward the blue unmarked police car.

Tucker jogged up behind them, and as she climbed into the passenger side, he leaned down to see the driver.

"Sarah, this is Eli Buchanan. Eli, Sarah."

She shook the man's hand once she settled into his car. He had dark brown hair and a brawny build, and though his smile was brief and guarded, she trusted Tucker and Heath's assessment that he would protect her.

"Eli is an FBI cyber special agent who works out of Erie, but he lives here. He offered his assistance when Heath told him what was going on. Eli is engaged to Molly, Heath's sister."

"Thank you for helping them today. And congratulations on your engagement. I'm surprised Heath allowed you near his sister." She tucked away a grin, and all three men chuckled.

"Thanks. My game plan was simple—win over Molly's heart. Then win over Heath." His smile fell. "My condolences about Tanner. I...know what that feels like."

"Thank you." Had Eli lost a spouse as well?

Tucker cleared his throat, then addressed Eli. "Heath and I will check out the bakery's perimeter with the other officer, see if we can locate the clothes."

Heath circled the car and spoke to Eli, and Tucker's gaze fell on Sarah.

"I'll see you in a few." He reached into the car and cupped her cheek briefly. The tenderness of his touch sent a flush across her skin.

"Please be careful."

Sarah watched as the men disappeared behind the bakery. Tucker had called the man who owned the business, and he'd given them the code to get inside if that became necessary. Tucker had his gun drawn, and he headed around the back of the store, which butted up against a cluster of trees. In the distance, the Allegheny River snaked through the edge of town, visible through the bare limbs and skeletal branches of the winterized forest.

She clasped her hands on her lap. "Tucker mentioned Molly is a forest ranger too."

"She's a botanist. She and my mom think planting gardens can heal all the world's problems." He snickered, then sobered up. "My daughter and I are blessed to have her in our lives."

"You have a child?" She turned to Eli. "How old is she?"

"Skylar is six. She's obsessed with these Breyer horses. It's all she wants for Christmas. Well, that and those bracelet kits. The ones with all the beads. She likes making them. See?" He held out his burly arm and pushed back his jacket sleeve. A colorful bracelet with blues, greens and purple encircled his veiny wrist. There were letters on it, but Sarah couldn't make them out.

"It has my initials, Molly's and hers." He beamed, then pushed his jacket back over his wrist and his light-hearted expression settled back to serious. "How old is your son?"

"Liam is seven."

Movement in Sarah's peripheral vision caught her attention. Eli noticed, too, because he grasped the gun on his lap and stared across the parking lot. The third police officer was peering in a bakery window on the right side of the building, but there was no sign of Tucker and Heath.

A man's shout carried across the lot, and then Tucker jogged over to Eli's car.

Sarah rolled the window down, and he leaned in, breathing hard. "We found the clothes, but it's a decoy. Heath just got a call that there was an attempted break-in at his house."

Her heart caught in her throat. The men were trying to get into Heath's house?

"Officer Venetta's there, right?" Eli asked.

"Yes. He tussled with the guy." Heath joined them as Tucker explained. "A masked man was seen on the side of Heath's house. When Officer Venetta approached, the man moved in aggressively. Venetta and the suspect fought, then the suspect took off through the neighborhood. Back up is on the way."

Sarah clutched the console. "What happened?"

"Three dogs happened, that's what," Heath growled as he shoved his gun in his holster. "The suspect disarmed the alarm by cutting my power, but he didn't realize there'd be a whole bunch of trained fangs inside."

"Is Officer Venetta okay?" Sarah asked.

"He has a bloody nose, but otherwise he's good. He's being checked out by paramedics," Heath responded, then motioned at Eli and Tucker. "I need to get over there."

Sarah stayed put, riding the ten minutes to Heath's house in silence with Eli. When they arrived, Tucker and Heath checked in with the EMTs as they finished up with Officer Venetta.

She stayed in Eli's unmarked car as Heath headed inside to check on his dogs. Eli, Tucker, and another officer walked through the yard and a nearby stand of trees searching for any signs of footprints. She noticed that Tucker hung back, keeping close to the driveway where she sat in the police car.

Finally, he trotted over to Eli's car, his features marred by a scowl.

"He was coming after me, wasn't he?" She hated how her words faltered.

Tucker reached back to massage his neck. "My guess would be yes. He assumed we'd head to the bakery to check for the clothes, which we did, but he thought you'd still be here. Thank the Lord you came along with us. Although, those three dogs in there would've protected you with their lives if you'd stayed behind."

Sarah rubbed her brows, careful not to touch the sore spot on her head. "I'm so glad Officer Venetta and the dogs are all okay." She dropped her hands. "I just want Liam. I want him found. And I don't want any of you hurt. Please, Lord, I need to find my son."

"Hey, Tuck! Check this out." Eli's voice cut through her feeble prayer. Sarah climbed out of Eli's car and stood next to Tucker. His arm came around her, and she leaned into him.

Heath loped out of his front door and joined them.

Eli held up a crumpled brochure. *Happy Moments Campground* was written in bold black letters across the top, and a wrinkled, faded image of a cabin filled the front page. "Our perp must've dropped this in the tussle."

"The campground," Tucker exclaimed, and Heath nodded. "They have Liam at the campground."

"Use me as bait." Sarah sat beside Tucker at the table, her posture slumped but her eyes bright and determined. "Please. Just tell me what to do."

Tucker blew out a hard breath. Why was she so eager to throw herself to the wolves? *Because she loves her son.* He couldn't argue with that reasoning, especially since he'd do the same thing in her situation.

Eli had gone home, the police report had been filed, and he, Sarah and Heath were sitting around Heath's kitchen table. The power had been restored, and the bright lights made Tucker's headache return.

Or maybe it was the idea of Sarah in grave danger that made his skull pound.

"You understand that we're only doing this because we are confident the suspects need you for something. Otherwise..." He dropped his gaze to the table.

"Otherwise, they'll just kill me."

He shuddered. "Exactly. We'll be there, too, but there will be a period of time you're on your own." He reached across the table, covering her clenched hands with one of his. "Nothing about this will be safe."

"I don't need safe," Sarah shot back. "I need my son."

Heath cleared his throat. "We can't go in now anyway. I need a few hours to gather a team. Let's get some rest tonight. We'll plan to hit the campground a little before dawn. I'll let you know when we're prepared and everything's in place."

"By the way, there's a construction and ranger maintenance road at the back of the campground," Tucker noted. "We'll need officers there. I would guess that's the road the suspects used to get in and out of the campgrounds. We rangers aren't active in that area this time of year. The campground is basically shut down."

Sarah flipped her hand, lining their palms together on the table, and he struggled to focus on the conversation.

"There's something else." She squeezed their fingers together. "Mr. Drake called earlier and left another message. I think you both should hear it."

She pulled out her cell with her free hand and set it on the table, then hit the voicemail button.

"Sarah, this is Alexander Drake. I need to speak with you

immediately. Officers recovered something in your house that we need to discuss. Please call me ASAP."

Heath stifled a yawn. "It's late, but you up for calling now?"

"Sure. Do I tell him you're both here or not?"

Tucker glanced at Heath, then Heath spoke. "I'd say err on the side of not mentioning it. If he asks, be honest. We can't use any information he tells us unless he knows we're listening."

She nodded, then hit the green call button on her cell. Two rings later, Alexander Drake answered in a scratchy voice. "Drake here."

"Mr. Drake, this is Sarah. I just got your message. I hope I'm not calling too late."

"Not a problem. Thank you for returning my call. How are you doing? Any news on your son?"

She shot a questioning look at Tucker, and he shook his head. "Not really. Authorities are still searching for him." Her voice was infused with genuine pain and fear. Tucker's heart went out to her.

"I'm sorry to hear that. I hope those monsters are caught and he's back with you soon."

"Thank you." She licked her lips, and Tucker's gaze alighted on the unconscious gesture before he yanked it away. "You said you needed to talk to me about something?"

"Right. Officers stumbled on a file folder your husband had placed in a locked drawer in his office. It was at the back of a filing cabinet."

They all exchanged surprised looks over the kitchen table.

"What did they find?" she inquired casually.

"It's paperwork about a group of physicians and scientists who...shall we say, do the opposite of what their code of conduct calls for. And the files the officer found seem to point to your husband's involvement with them."

"I don't understand. Tanner wasn't a doctor or scientist."

"Correct, but he oversaw the creation and implementation of a powerful new drug, working in tandem with scientists and doctors. As you know, this drug could change—improve—the lives of many older adults struggling with Parkinson's." Mr. Drake moved, and the phone made a staticky noise.

"What group are you talking about?"

"I believe Tanner was involved with the DSU."

"What does that mean, those letters?"

"Doctors Scientists Underground. They are a dangerous collection of law-breaking individuals who fleece the international pharmaceutical industry."

Sarah met Tucker's eyes, then he tugged out his cell and typed the name into the search engine. Heath edged closer, reading over his shoulder. Then they set the phone in front of her.

Doctors Scientists Underground was founded in 2014 in Geneva and included dozens of members worldwide. The FBI and CIA had been unable to pin down an official number of participants in the DSU, other than occasional arrests. According to the website, nearly all those involved remained in the dark about the DSU members, which kept government officials on tenterhooks trying to tie those arrested to the actual group. The DSU was involved in hundreds of black-market deals for medicine, both FDA approved and not, resulting in net earnings upward of nearly twelve billion dollars annually.

"Do you know for sure Tanner was part of it?" she asked breathlessly.

"I don't know for certain, other than he was in possession of incriminating paperwork that connects him to the DSU." As Mr. Drake spoke, Tucker thought of a question she could ask him and scribbled it on a pad of paper.

Drake continued, "The DSU obtains pre-FDA approved, as

well as rejected, medications and vaccines for the purposes of selling them on the international black market."

Sarah leaned over, her hair tickling Tucker's chin as she read Tucker's question. "Mr. Drake, do you think Mark Sousa is part of this too?"

Drake harrumphed. "I'm not certain, but I have a feeling he is."

"Okay," she answered, and her eyes flew up to Tucker's again. "Mr. Drake, thank you for letting me know about this. I'm sorry, but I've never heard of the DSU or heard Tanner talk about it."

"I wouldn't expect so, as you're not involved in this industry like I am."

Sarah rolled her eyes at the man's arrogance, and Tucker grinned. She stuck her tongue out at him, and Tucker couldn't pull his gaze from her playful expression and how it transformed her face.

How he wanted to get her laughing again. Often. All the time. Which started with finding Liam.

Heath smacked Tucker's arm, bringing Tucker back to reality. Pieces were falling into place. If what Alexander Drake said was true, Tanner had gotten involved with a dangerous group of white-collar, high-society criminals, and Sarah unintentionally had landed in the middle of the fray.

Unfortunately, that meant these men would stop at nothing to get to her, leaving them with little choice but to do what she asked to get her son back…

Use her as bait.

THIRTEEN

Sarah ran her fingers through her damp, clean hair. She stood in front of the mirror in Heath's second-floor guest room, a fresh bandage applied to her forehead. At least she was somewhat presentable after getting cleaned up.

"Mroaw." Mr. Meow figure-eighted around her ankles, and she crouched to love on him. His collar was now evidence at the police station, and it felt strange petting him without it on. Stranger still to be around the cat without Liam.

Please, God. Bring him back to me.

Tucker had driven out to his house to meet a contractor about repairing the damaged corner of his garage and the gaping back door, and he'd asked her to stay at Heath's with Eli, his fiancée, Molly, Eli's daughter, Skylar, and Heath's daughter, Piper.

"Liam should be doing this." She lifted the hefty feline and pressed a kiss to his soft head. "You miss him, too, don't you? We'll get our boy back soon. Please, Lord." She tested the words, then closed her eyes. "God, I...want to trust You like Tucker does. I want to believe You can forgive me like he says you can." Her throat thickened so she had to whisper the words. "Help me believe, God. Give me the faith to trust You."

A soft knock came from the closed door. She draped Mr. Meow across one arm, then opened it with the other. Molly

Calhoun stood in the hallway. She was tall and slender, with shoulder-length auburn hair and honey-colored eyes, her bone structure a feminized version of Heath's. Her natural beauty was enhanced by the welcoming smile Molly always seemed to wear.

"Hi, well, look at you, kitty." She petted the cat, then met Sarah's eyes. "Did you want me to put the other half of your calzone in the fridge?"

Molly must've noticed she hadn't eaten much of it. They'd gotten a huge to-go order at a local Italian restaurant. Pizza for the kids and calzones for the adults. So much food, and Liam wasn't there to share any of it.

"Sure, thank you. I don't have much of an appetite right now." Sarah backtracked into the guest bedroom, then set Mr. Meow down on the round braided rug beside the bed. He crouched and contemplated the open door, until Molly stepped inside and closed it.

"No escaping, kitty." Molly wagged a finger at him.

"Good idea." Sarah sat atop the guest bed. "He wants to explore the house pretty badly."

"The dogs wouldn't hurt you, but I can't guarantee they won't chase you," Molly crooned to Mr. Meow as he circled her ankles. She crouched to pet him once more.

"About the food—I'm sorry, I just can't stomach much right now. I'm not sure they're even feeding Liam." A sob threatened. "How can *I* eat when he may not be?"

Molly hurried over and sat beside her. "It's all right. I didn't mean to push you about it. Heath and Tucker are very focused on finding him. They seem confident that his kidnappers have him at the Happy Moments Campground."

"I'm grateful for them. And I pray they're right." Her body suddenly felt too heavy to keep upright. "Poor Tucker. His house is messed up. His garage. He lost some of his beautiful carvings, all because of the men coming after me."

"Trust me, he's not upset about it. I mean, he doesn't like that it happened. But Tucker knows what's truly important in life. He cares about you, about your safety."

"Yeah, that's what he said, but I still feel bad for disrupting his life like this, especially after he lost his brother."

"Tucker is glad to be helping you and Liam. He's one of the good guys, for sure."

Sarah's chest burned a little at the familiar way Molly spoke his name and the fondness in her expression.

Stop it. Molly is engaged to Eli. The three blind mice could see their love and devotion for each other.

Still, she couldn't help wondering about Molly and Tucker. "You two work together and…know each other pretty well?"

"Me and Tucker? We've been working together a few years through the forest service. He's got my back, and I've got his. Other than Eli and my brother, he's one of the best men I know."

Sarah tilted her head. "Tucker admires you too. Why…" Was she overstepping by asking? "Why didn't you two date?"

"Tucker?" Molly dragged out his name with a sour face. "Sure, he's good looking, but yuck, we're like siblings. Besides," she said slyly, "he's held a candle for this one girl for so long no other woman has measured up."

Sarah's stomach sank. Was this the high school girlfriend Tanner had mentioned years ago? The one who had moved away?

Sarah's thoughts returned to last night at Tucker's house. "There's this paramedic, Marcy, who seemed to be sweet on him."

"Oh, right. Marcy. Yeah, she—"

Someone knocked on the door, interrupting them. Eli appeared. "Hey, hon, you two going to join us? Heath wants to decorate his tree and get everyone to bed early enough so we can all function tomorrow."

"You're going tomorrow too?" Molly launched at Eli, and Sarah tried not to stare as they embraced and shared a brief kiss. Their affection for each other brought a lump to her throat.

Molly extricated herself and turned to Sarah. "You want to string some popcorn and help us hang ornaments?"

No. I just want my son. But she needed to do something other than mope and fret.

Sarah swiped her hands down the black leggings she'd borrowed from Molly. "Let's do it."

Ten minutes later, she sat cross-legged on the carpet in Heath's living room. Piper and Skylar worked on a box of ornaments, discussing and describing each ornament to each other in excited voices, while Eli and Molly oversaw placing the extra strings of lights on the tree. Sarah, on the other hand, had been given the job of stringing popcorn. A great idea, because it kept her mind focused on the task and not on how much she missed Liam.

Finite handiwork was not her forte. Twice, she poked her fingertip, drawing a tiny bead of blood.

"May I help?"

Tucker. She looked up into his blue eyes, and her heart double-thumped. Then she remembered what Molly had said about the woman Tucker still cared about, and she wilted.

"Sure."

He grabbed a tissue from the box on the end table, then crouched beside her. Gently pressing it to her finger, he used the tissue to wipe the dollop of blood away, his strong forearms and large fingers deftly cradling hers. In her peripheral vision, the tiny dark dots of his beard covered his cheek, and the sudden urge to feel the smooth roughness of his skin surprised her.

He glanced her way, and their eyes met. She noted the worry lines and depth of unease in his blue eyes.

"What is it?" she asked softly.

"I called my mom on the drive over."

"Oh, Tucker." She longed to wrap her arms around him, show him that she cared, that she understood. Instead, she put her threaded needle down and touched his knee. "How did Sharlene take it?"

"Aunt Nell had already told her." He grabbed a few pieces of popcorn and nudged the needle tip through them. "She's upset, understandably pretty emotional, but her focus is like mine. Like ours. Finding her grandson."

She pulled her arm back. "I'm really glad Aunt Nell is there with her."

"Me too." Still, an undercurrent of tension marked his words, and she watched him carefully as he stabbed a few kernels that crumbled under his stiff grasp.

"Hey, is there something else?" She covered his hand with her own.

"I don't want you going tomorrow," he muttered.

"I have to. You know I do. I'll be okay. You'll be there."

"I don't want to lose you again."

"Uncle Tuck, do you like the horse or the mermaid ornament better?" Piper asked.

Tucker gave her hand a gentle squeeze, then stood. Sarah's thoughts exploded then converged as she considered Tucker's whispered words.

I don't want to lose you again. Had she heard him correctly? Did he mean as his friend and former sister-in-law—or as more?

"That's a tough call," Tucker rubbed his chin as he pretended to think deeply about Piper's question. "But I think I'll go with the horse since I don't swim very well. Now, Miss Sarah here, she swims like a fish." He winked down at her. "She was so good she swam in the Olympics, where they win those big medals, then they hang them around their necks while they're standing on a podium."

"What?" Piper practically screamed. "In the big pool?"

Sarah met Tucker's playful smile, and she couldn't help returning one. He'd probably misspoken and meant he didn't want to lose her, too, like he'd lost Tanner.

"I did swim in that big pool," she acknowledged.

"Did you beat everybody in the whole world to get there?"

"Uh…" She shot Tucker a *Look What You Started* smile. "Maybe not *everyone*."

"She only lost by like one-one-hundredth of a second," Tucker noted. "She got silver. So, second place. But she was a winner in a relay race, when four swimmers swim together."

"So you're the grand champion!" Piper squealed.

Skylar joined in. "She's a grand champion in the big pool!"

Heath entered the fray. "Why are we yelling about pools at Christmastime?"

"Because Miss Sarah is a grand champion, Daddy. She won all the medals."

"Piper, don't exaggerate. While I'm sure Ms. Sarah would've loved to win all the medals, that's impossible." Heath tussled his daughter's hair, and then he herded the exuberant, sugar-fueled girls back to the ornament box. He turned to Sarah. "Thanks for sacrificing your hands for the popcorn strands. They look great."

"I see how it is. You gave the newbie the hardest job," she teased back.

"Nah, I have it on good authority you're the toughest of all of us. Tucker told me once you, he, and Tanner had a pull-up contest and you won."

She shrugged. "Back then I was fifteen pounds lighter and a lot stronger."

Heath cracked a grin, then headed over to his daughter.

"You're even more beautiful now than you were then," Tucker said softly.

Her eyes widened. Tanner had rarely said much about her physical appearance, especially in the last two years, and Tucker's sincere praise was a balm to her heart.

"C'mon, let's get this popcorn up, then get some rest. Heath said four-thirty we head to the campgrounds."

They carefully stepped over the girls and the half-emptied boxes of bright green, red and blue items. Heath's seven-foot-Fraser fir stood proudly dressed in front of his picture window, a sparkling reflection doubling the beauty. She noted that Tucker placed himself between herself and the window as they readied to wrap the popcorn strands around the tree.

Reaching out his long arms, Tucker squatted, stretching the first strand along the tree's base then handing it to Sarah. She clasped it, unable to ignore the heat that shot from his fingertips to hers. Warmth climbed her neck. By the third time, halfway up the tree, his touch lingered on hers, and she had to focus to spread the strand evenly.

Finally, they finished, and he stepped away from the back of the tree. Heath, Molly, Eli and the girls headed to the kitchen for hot chocolate, but Sarah and Tucker remained in the living room.

"It's so pretty." She gazed at the tree for several seconds, then glanced at Tucker. He was watching her instead, his eyes reflecting the sparkling lights with a solemnity she felt herself drowning in. "I wish Liam could see it too."

"He will. Soon." Tucker's calm assurance comforted her as she took in the colorful tree.

Please, God, I pray Tucker is right. I can't face Christmas without Liam.

Tucker climbed into the front seat of Eli's unmarked car, his mind returning to the nightmare that had tortured his restless sleep. Sarah, caught by the men who had killed Tanner.

She sat in the back, and Heath drove separate from them in his squad car. Two additional Holloway officers would be stationed at the ranger entrance to Happy Moments Campground, which was situated at the back of the four-hundred-acre camping, hiking and boating area set on the edge of Allegheny National Forest.

He turned and met Sarah's eyes. "Get any sleep?"

"Not much." She swallowed, her pale throat bobbing. "You?"

"Maybe four hours. It'll be enough." He faced the front again, not about to tell her that he could kick himself for what he'd said to her last night, or how much he was second-guessing having Sarah involved in this at all.

I don't want to lose you again.

Foolish. She could've chosen him years ago, but she'd chosen Tanner instead. Now she was newly widowed and distraught over her son's kidnapping. This was no time to consider what might be between them, and he wasn't sure he wanted to in the future. He couldn't risk his heart again if she didn't care about him like he did for her.

"I just want to hold my son. I want him safe. I want to go home."

Tucker's pulse flickered. Home to Fountain View. Five hours away. Another reason things wouldn't—couldn't—work out with them.

Onyx whined in the back, his energy levels sky-high. The dog sensed Tucker's emotions and fed off them, and Tucker worked to keep his adrenaline calm.

Too quickly, they arrived at a friend's house, who agreed to let them gather behind his home. Heath pulled in right after them. Manny Alvarez lived about a quarter mile from the entrance to Happy Moments Campground. Manny's wife, Gina, had been Piper's second-grade teacher, and Manny and Heath played on the local softball team in the spring. Manny's house would conceal the two vehicles as they continued on foot.

"You're sure you're up for this?" Tucker asked.

"Yes. I want to do this." She had steel in her voice, and Tucker's respect for her rose even higher. What a brave woman. Brave mother.

"It's about a mile drive. You'll take Heath's extra car." He explained which way she'd go. "I don't know how long it will be until the men see you."

And you're temporarily at their mercy—or lack of.

"I'm ready." Sarah's voice was steely, and after they parked, she was the first one out of the car. She adjusted her sweatshirt, tugging at the Kevlar vest Heath had lent her and Tucker had made her wear.

"I'm sorry if that's uncomfortable, but you need to keep it on." He came up next to her, longing to pull her into his arms and tell her everything would be okay. Longing to promise her that they would find Liam and get her and her son to safety. But none of that was certain.

The only thing certain in this situation was that God was with them.

Manny exited his house, a steaming cup of coffee in hand. Gina stood in the window, offering a brief wave while wearing a worried expression.

"Can we pray first?" Tucker asked Heath when he strode

over, and the four of them plus Manny huddled together as Tucker poured out his heart.

"Father in Heaven, you know exactly where Liam is. Guide us to him. Please keep Sarah and the rest of the team safe. We trust in You. In Jesus's name, amen."

They all whispered *Amen*, and Tucker lifted his gaze to find Sarah regarding him with a tender expression. She mouthed, *Thank you*, and he nodded back.

"Tuck, you all set?" Heath checked the earpiece in Tucker's ear. "You can hear me okay?" He checked his own earpiece. "Testing. Testing."

Five minutes later, Sarah drove away in Heath's older-model SUV. Tucker made sure Heath had a tracking device on her, and they'd notified the Pennsylvania State Police of the situation. Two PSP deputies were stationed as backup near the ranger entrance road, and one was hidden among a cluster of trees in a driveway just south of the campground.

Dirty snow crunched underfoot as he and Onyx crossed the road and bisected a field. His partner was raring to go. They would swing south of the main path, keeping her within a hundred yards but staying hidden in the trees below the paved roadway leading into the campground.

Normally, being outdoors calmed him. He loved these woods, loved this forest he called home and spent so much time in. But today he was alert to every owl's hoot and each snap of twigs underfoot. It was still pitch dark, and his sense of direction lead him forward. Onyx tugged at his leash, eager for a run and brimming with energy. At first, Tucker caught a glimpse of Heath's car as it drove down the winding lane toward the campground, but for the most part he—and Sarah—were on their own.

God, please protect her. Please help us get Liam back safely.

Three minutes later, he and Onyx ended up about five hundred yards from the campground.

Suddenly, Sarah's quiet voice came over the earpiece. "I'm here. I parked in front of the main building. I'm getting out on foot. Go left?" she asked.

"Yes. Hang left in about a hundred yards. Past the main office. Follow the road. There's a pool and a playground. Go past all that." They'd discussed how the men were likely holed up near the back of the empty campground. It made more sense to assume that. "But keep an eye out. And remember our code words for when you see them."

"It's so cold out, where is my son?" Sarah returned verbatim. They'd come up with a code for her upon seeing the men that was somewhat sensical so the men wouldn't suspect she was in communication with anyone else.

"Listen, Sarah," Tucker murmured as he trudged through the ravine that edged the Allegheny River. "I know you can't see me. But I'm close. You're not alone."

"I'm glad I can hear you," she whispered. "I'm walking past the campground office now. I can't talk anymore. Please pray."

"Men are in position," Heath's rough, low voice interjected.

Sarah's plea for prayer twisted Tucker's heart. He leaped over a small creek, a tributary of the Allegheny, his boots sloshing in the icy mud. Onyx sprang over the water like a deer, his muscles bunching beneath his black coat.

He couldn't stand the thought that these men might kill her before he could—what? Before he could...

Before I tell her I love her. Of course, he loved her. He always had, always would.

Tanner was gone. But Tucker was here, and he would do everything in his power to keep Sarah safe and get Liam back to her. Even if she didn't love him that way in return, he needed to see Sarah smiling again.

Suddenly, Sarah gasped, and the crackle of motion in his ear froze him to the earth.

"Well, look who's here," a male voice snarled. "You musta got my note."

"It's so cold out, where is my son?" she said shakily.

More scuffling came over the earpiece, then a loud *whack* filled Tucker's ear. His muscles twitched as he waited with bated breath for any more noise.

"You get that?" Heath's voice cut in.

"Check her for bugs. See, look at her ear. Shut that—"

Silence screamed through Tucker's earpiece, and he started running toward the campground, Onyx racing out ahead.

FOURTEEN

Sarah awoke to the sensation of being dragged over cold, hard ground. A hand cinched around her ankles, and pain splintered down her legs as her spine cracked into a solid surface—a rock? Stump? Icy dampness seeped through the light snow pants Molly had lent her, and her shirt bunched up around her waist. Where was her jacket?

A scream throttled her throat. The men had come out from behind a utility shed. How had they known she would be there?

"Here. Your turn." The grip on her ankle released, and her leg crashed to the ground, her muscles pitifully useless. Where was Liam?

The second man let out a curse, then grabbed her ankle roughly. "How much further?"

"It's up here. You telling me you're lost already?"

"These places all look the same," the second man grumbled. "Where we taking sleeping beauty?"

Sarah flinched at the smirking comment, but she pretended to still be out. She didn't want them to know she was awake.

God, please help me be strong. I need my son.

"There. Finally."

From her position on the ground, with her eyes mostly slit shut, it was tough to make out her surroundings. The campsites seemed to alternate for RV hookup space and a small cabin, and the men appeared to be staying in a cabin. On closer inspection, she noticed there was no car parked nearby, and a sign in the cabin's front said *Closed for Remodel*.

Was that how they stayed out of the forest rangers' radar? Where was their car?

She adjusted her arm against her side to test if the vest Tucker had put on her was still in place. It was so tight it must not have moved. If they decided to shoot her in the head...

She folded her lips in and moaned.

"Did you hear that? She's coming around."

She moaned again and moved her head, keeping her eyes closed so they'd believe she was completely out. How far away were Tucker and the other officers? Her instincts told her to keep still. Especially since her endgame was seeing Liam.

"She's out, man. Just bring her inside."

A pair of thick arms scooped under her, and then she bumped against a male's burly chest. The cloying scent of body odor and bologna stung her nose, the man's acrid smell and his overwhelming proximity igniting a long-buried memory of Jack, one of her mom's abusive boyfriends from her teenaged years. Jack had tried to hurt her one night when her mom was working late. Sarah struggled against the fight or flight urge compelling her to get away. To get to safety.

No. She needed to see Liam, needed to hold him, so she forced her stricken muscles to obey. *Please, God.*

"Mommy!"

Liam. His voice was the most beautiful sound she'd ever heard. "Liam! I'm here, baby, I'm here."

"Hurry, man. Get her inside, now."

She tried to look around, but the heavyset man lugging her forward grabbed her around the waist and half carried, half dragged her toward a back room.

"Shut it, lady. Just..." He shoved her down onto a chair in a small bedroom, then proceeded to loop rope around her wrists and tied them to the armrests.

"Where is my son? I need to see him." A thought struck. Even if Tucker and the men could still hear her, how would they know which cabin to go in? There were over a dozen in the area, and once they entered one, wouldn't their cover be blown?

"Mommy?"

Where was he? "I'm here, baby. I'll see you soon."

"You can see him now." Suddenly, the burly man reappeared, holding a small—

"Liam!" Fireworks broke out in her chest, blinding her as joyous tears drenched her face. If only her wrists weren't tied so she could hug him. Press him to her, heart-to-heart.

"I'm so sorry," she sobbed as the man set Liam in a chair beside her. "Are you hurt?"

"My toe got stubbed. I don't like it here. Mommy, you don't have to cry. They said they wanted you to open the thingy. Is Mr. Meow okay?" His precious little voice morphed from steady to sad. "That big man put something in his collar, then they pushed him out of the car."

"Mr. Meow is safe." Sarah lowered her voice so the men couldn't catch what she said. "There's a sweet little girl watching him right now until we get back."

"A girl? He's with a *girl*? Oh, man."

Sarah couldn't help smiling. She wiggled her wrists again to test the rope. "Have you eaten anything?"

"Yeah, but it was a sandwich with yucky pink stuff on it. And some water."

Thank You, Lord. Her greatest fear was her son not eating, not being cared for, yet God had seen to Liam's needs. "I'm glad you got to eat and drink something."

It was dark, and it was hard to make out her son's features clearly in the shadowy room.

Liam's random comment from a moment ago circled back in her thoughts. *They said they wanted you to open the thingy.*

"You said the men want me to open something?"

"I dunno, yeah I guess."

The men's voices carried over from the main area of the cabin, one increasingly angry, the other appeasing.

"They do that a lot. Fight. Like you and Daddy."

Tanner. She tucked her chin. He didn't know about Tanner.

"Mommy, I have something bad to tell you."

Her stomach, already tied in knots about their dire circumstances, dropped to her shoes.

"That bad man out there, one of them is called Davy, he said Daddy was dead."

Sarah's heart constricted. Liam must've overheard something and asked about Tanner. *Lord, please help me say this right.*

"Is that true?" Liam's voice broke.

Even under these terrible circumstances, she couldn't lie to him. "Yes, baby, I'm so sorry, it is true. Someone hurt him at work, and he died. I hope you know Daddy loves…loved… you so much, and he—"

"Hey! I hear you two talking in there. That's enough." The louder, burlier man—Davy, according to her son—darkened the doorway. "If you think that cop and the forest ranger guy will find you, you're wrong. Where we're going, they won't be able to follow."

He lumbered away from her view, and Sarah inched her legs out so her shoes brushed her son's leg. She desperately needed to touch him, hold him close. At least she could see him.

"What's going to happen, Mommy?"

A measure of assurance filled her as she considered Tucker, Heath and the other law enforcement out there in the woods.

"Your uncle Tucker and some police officers are coming to save us." *Please, Lord, let it be true.*

Suddenly, a large form reappeared in the doorway. "Let's go."

As the smaller man yanked her upright, two nagging questions pinpointed in her mind. Where were they taking her and Liam? And what did these men want her to open?

Tucker slid between the row of trees hedging the cabin. In one hand he clasped his weapon and in the other Onyx's shortened lead. Darkness still held the campground in its grip, and the air had a bite to it that made his bones ache. In only a half an hour, the sun would appear over the horizon, and they hoped to catch these killers before the rest of the world woke up.

Onyx had tracked Sarah with the shirt he'd brought along, and the dog stood sentry beside him, his ears perked as he panted softly. Tucker had taken off in a sprint after hearing Sarah's scream. Good thing his idea of a sprint was an easy lope for Onyx.

He bent over to check the bandage on Onyx's leg. Despite the superficial wound, the K9 was just getting started, energy-wise.

"Location?"

Heath's voice blasted in Tucker's ear. Every time someone spoke into the earpiece, it interfered with his hearing aid, and the feedback crackled like lightning zapping an electrical box.

"I'm in. You?"

"Backup position."

"Ten-four. Going in."

Tucker crept forward, Onyx flanking him. He couldn't help

thinking back to the attack at the ranger station months ago, where two cyber criminals chasing Eli had attempted to destroy evidence from a shooting on the river. In the process, Tucker had found himself outnumbered and outgunned. Eli and Molly had stopped by the ranger station that day and had found him.

Never again. Part of the reason he'd jumped at the opportunity to have a K9 partner was for this very reason. An extra set of ears and extra set of eyes. A bunch of sharp teeth.

"You ready, boy?"

Onyx whined, his light brown eyes shining with eagerness and focus. What a partner.

The campsite was eerily silent, and in the darkness, Tucker noted the lack of vehicles. No campers, no vehicles. Surely the men had driven here, but where was their car?

Before they arrived, Tucker and Heath found out that there were thirty-four camping spots in this area and another fifteen a few hundred yards away, edging the lake. Several were under construction, a few being renovated, though that had been halted until spring. Happy Moments Director Richard White had given them a plethora of information when they called late last night, including the fact that the campgrounds were technically closed this time of year, but he did have one person checked in.

Some years we don't have any visitors from Thanksgiving to New Year's Day, Richard had said. *Then they come in January to cross-country ski, snowshoe or snowmobile.*

The single cabin in use was reserved by Timothy Bashaw, from Savannah, Georgia, a name that sounded vaguely familiar. Heath was obtaining a warrant to secure the full name and information about the campground user.

Tucker strode quietly up an incline that fed directly into the main road leading to the back of the campground. He kept to the tree line, his pace urgent but steps careful. The air stung his eyes and nose, and his breath plumed out in time with his racing heart.

Christmas was days away. Of all the situations he'd expected this year, never would he have believed that Sarah would return to Holloway. Or that Tanner would be killed. Or that he'd be part of a team hunting down armed suspects holding his nephew hostage.

As Tucker approached the main building, his gaze combed the ground. Sarah had relayed that she saw the building shortly before she screamed. She'd been near this spot. Onyx strained on his leash, alternating snuffling the ground and then sniffing the air. Tucker gripped the cold metal of his weapon, his nerves firing with every twig crunch and *woosh* of the wind.

He loped up to the front doors of the main building. Low shrubs sat on either side of the double doors, and dark glass covered what was inside. Richard White had mentioned a spare key, but it didn't appear that anyone was inside the main building.

"See anything?" Heath's voice crackled in Tucker's ear.

"Nothing. No tracks. But Onyx seems to be following a trail."

Tucker edged around the brick building then treaded back onto the campground's main driveway.

"Here, boy." He held Sarah's shirt out again, and Onyx pressed his muzzle into it, then set off at trot. Tucker increased his pace to keep up. Ahead of them sat a small cabin, followed by a large open space with a hookup. Beyond that another cabin materialized out of the darkness. Every other spot was a cabin beside an RV hookup, in case families wanted to bring an RV and use the cabin facilities.

Suddenly, Onyx lunged forward, yanking the leash.

"Easy boy," Tucker panted as he struggled to keep up. The

leash extended several yards, and Onyx reached the end as he darted down the lane heading deeper into the campsite.

After crossing three sets of cabin and RV hookups, Tucker whistled softly to Onyx and regained control of the leash. They had to be close. A few hundred more yards, then they'd reach the end of the first campground.

They passed down the row of cabins plus RV hookups, then Onyx aimed for one in particular. Tucker reined him in closer and took in the surroundings. A newer red sedan was parked beside the cabin, and the ground around the structure was littered with shoe treads. He slunk toward a grill beside the cabin, and pressed a hand on it. Cold. Hadn't been used recently. Onyx snuffled around the stairs, where a plastic bag lay crumpled on the ground. A potato-chip bag. Looked fresh.

A dark lump of material caught his eye, shoved beside the front step. Onyx tugged him toward it. Was that...

His blood pressure spiked. Sarah's navy jacket lay on the ground in a heap. Onyx snuffled the material, then sat.

"Good boy," Tucker whispered. "We're not done."

He took the three steps in one leap, his weapon ready, and rapped on the front door. Onyx hugged his side. "This is the police. Identify yourself."

Several seconds passed as he waited, his muscles like rope and heart thudding in his ears. The sound of shuffling footsteps and a man's irritated voice carried through the door.

The knob turned, and Tucker tightened his grip on the gun. Onyx whined, pressing into Tucker's left leg. He was learning his partner did that to regulate himself before an attack.

"Easy, boy."

The door swung open, and a heavyset, balding man with a thick gray beard wearing a pair of flannel pajamas stood in the doorway. He took one look at Onyx and Tucker, and his eyes flew open. Both palms stuck up in the air.

"Whoa, whoa. Officer, I didn't do anything."

"Identify yourself."

"Tim Bashaw. Please don't shoot me."

"My name's Tucker Brindley. I'm a law enforcement ranger with the US Forest Service. I'm not going to shoot you. I do, however, need you to cooperate as I check your cabin. We just found an article of clothing belonging to a missing woman out front of this cabin."

"What? There's been no one here besides me for days."

The man—Mr. Bashaw—opened the door the rest of the way and floundered back, holding his hands up. He followed Onyx with wary, fascinated eyes as Tucker skimmed through the front room, small kitchen, then strode back to the single bedroom and a tiny laundry room near the back of the structure. No sign of anyone else. Blinds were drawn shut, and the air temperature was cooler than Tucker preferred. Maybe mid-fifties.

"Mind sharing what you're doing camping in Northwestern Pennsylvania in December?" Tucker's gut told him Mr. Bashaw, who looked about mid-sixties, was harmless. But he'd learned never to let down his guard, and Sarah's jacket was evidence enough her captors had been nearby in the last ten minutes.

"I'll tell you why I'm here, but you can't make this public."

Tucker's head whipped around. "Excuse me?"

Onyx felt the tension return to Tucker's body, and he rose to his haunches with a low growl.

Mr. Bashaw used a pointer finger to push up his glasses. "Look, I came here because I'm under contract."

"Explain." The man certainly didn't look like a contracted killer, but Tucker raised his brows and waited. The feed should be going through to the other officers standing sentry.

"I'm an author. I have a book due January fifteenth. I've

had writer's block, if you must know. It's the worst. The words just won't come out."

Writer's block? "What's this story called?"

He puffed out his chest. "My book is called *The Ice Man Returns*. It's the third book in a trilogy. Tales of the Ice Man. Ever heard of it?"

"I'm sorry, I can't say I have, but I'm not a big reader."

"Look, if you don't believe me, you can check my computer. Oh no, wait. You don't need to take it, do you? Hold on, let me save it one more time." Bashaw scurried to the kitchen table, where a laptop sat open, several books splayed beside it. A stack of papers was strewn across the table like a fan blew them that way. He showed Tucker his hands before clicking the mouse. "Please. I have no idea how that jacket got there. I only have fifteen thousand more words to go. I can't lose my laptop now."

Tucker scowled. He didn't have time for this. He needed to find Sarah. "Look, we're checking the campground for two or possibly three suspects who kidnapped a child."

The man's eyes widened again, making them as large as eggs behind his glasses. "Really?"

"Yes. I need to know if you've seen or heard anyone else here coming or going. Or seen any unusual behavior."

Mr. Bashaw patted the sparse hair on his head. "I did see a man driving a black minivan yesterday...no, two days ago? I'm not sure. The days run into each other when you're creatively engaged."

Tucker almost rolled his eyes at the man's dramatics. "Okay, did you get a look at the driver's or passenger's faces?"

"Not really. I heard the gravel crunching and had just started writing. It was bothersome, you know? I came here for cold temperatures and quiet. I needed it to be like a silent forest in winter." He gestured to the door. "But I only saw taillights."

"Great. Thanks." Tucker didn't bother hiding his sarcasm. No point in wasting any more time with Mr. Bashaw. Clearly, the men who had nabbed Sarah had planted the jacket to create a dummy trail.

Onyx growled, leaping toward the door.

"Easy boy." Tucker moved toward the entrance. The wind moaned outside, carrying through the cabin's notched-wall frame.

"Either myself or another officer will need to officially question you about what you've seen and heard, but we'll have to do that—"

The *thwack, whomp* of bullets piercing wood cut off Tucker's sentence. "Get down!" he shouted at Mr. Bashaw. The man jumped for the space behind the couch with a grunt, half falling and half scrambling for cover.

"Shots fired! I repeat, shots fired!"

"We're coming in," Heath's voice blasted over the earpiece.

Tucker crawled through the cabin, speaking to Mr. Bashaw as he did. "Stay down there until an officer comes in and gives you the clear."

"I'm not moving an inch." Mr. Bashaw's voice held a strange combination of fear and excitement, and Tucker spared one more look at him.

"You okay?"

"This is actually great stuff. You just gave me an idea for the last scene of my book."

Tucker shook his head, then inched toward the door. What a strange man. Who could think about a story at a time like this?

He glanced at the back of the cabin. Through the laundry and utility room, he'd glimpsed another door. Some of the cabins had back decks. Right now, this was his best option.

Tucker tightened the lead rope and beelined for the back door. He unclicked the lock and swung out the door, Onyx his shadow. The cover of dark worked both ways. It protected his movements but also hid the movements of the shooter.

Tucker flew down the back deck steps and rounded the building. Onyx lunged forward, and Tucker let the dog have his head. They burst through the bushes, and the dog barreled toward a cluster of oak trees. The element of surprise coupled with his stealthy speed gave Onyx the advantage, and in an instant the dog launched through the air. Straight for the shooter's gun arm. The man let out a shriek and fell backward, kicking out and writhing.

"Get him off me!" The shooter's screams split the early-morning air, and Tucker circled the suspect, handcuffs swinging while also casing the area to see if the man was alone.

A feminine scream tore through the night, followed by his name. He jerked upright.

"Tucker!"

FIFTEEN

Sarah cried out as the man forced them away from the cabin. The larger of the two men had left minutes ago, she assumed to go after Tucker, then the second man had dragged her and Liam at gunpoint outside. She blinked at the muted dawn surrounding them as a shiver coursed down her back. They'd taken her jacket, and her long-sleeved shirt offered little protection.

Even the Kevlar vest felt cold over the tank top below it.

"Don't make a sound." The gunman's eyes gleamed with hatred.

"What do you want from me?"

He yanked her arm again. "Your husband has some things we need. And you're going to help us get them."

"What things?" She tripped over a tree root. Were they looking for items connected to the group Alexander Drake had talked about—the DSU? Did they work for the Doctors Scientists Underground? "I have no idea what you're talking about."

"I think you do." Another tug, this one leading them away from the cabin and down a small incline.

"Mommy, it's cold."

"I know, baby." She wrapped her arm around his small body. When the men had taken his pajamas to put in her car, they'd made him change into an oversized man's shirt and a pair of sweatpants rolled-up at the waist that probably would've fit her.

Out of the corner of her eye, water glittered in the distance. A lake. From somewhere behind them burst a volley of barking, followed by a succession of snarling and pained shouts, carrying through the trees. *Onyx*. Tucker must be close.

Their captor spit out a colorful oath, then shoved her. "Get moving, lady."

"My son needs a jacket. Can I just—"

"No! Move."

They half ran, half stumbled down a descending trail that opened into the wide lake she'd seen. It shimmered under the remaining moonlight. Normally, the sight of water calmed her. But not today. Today the ice-rimmed shoreline sent a shiver down her spine.

The large wooden boat dock lay empty, except for a single speedboat. Recognition slapped her. Had the men been using the watercraft to get back and forth to Holloway, and hiding their car in another spot? No wonder there wasn't a car parked at the cabin they'd taken over.

"This way." Their captor jabbed her back with the weapon, and she flinched as the metal scraped her skin. She angled her head to try to watch what the man was doing. He kept looking back. He must've heard the dog's barking too.

Tucker. She had to tell him where they were. Otherwise, their captor would get them onto the boat, and they'd be lost on the enormous lake, which had numerous docking points throughout Allegheny National Forest.

"Where are you taking us?"

"I said stop talking and move!" The man whipped around and backhanded her. Stars burst in her vision, and she folded into herself at the instant, blinding pain in her mouth and the metallic taste of blood infiltrating her mouth.

"Don't hit my mom!" Liam pushed off her and body-slammed into their captor. Her son didn't weigh much, but the element of surprise was on his side, and their captor careened backward into a cluster of bushes.

Sarah hurried over to Liam and pulled her son away from the man as blood trickled down her chin and stung her split lip. "Shh. Calm down. We're going to be alright."

Please, Lord, let it be true.

"But he hit you."

"You little punk." The man righted himself and re-aimed the gun at her chest. "Get in the boat!"

"Okay, okay. We're moving." She caught Liam's wrists and herded him forward, placing herself between him and the angry gunman. "Baby, I'll go first."

"No, Mommy. I don't think we should go on that."

Their captor let out an impatient oath and lifted Sarah, tossing her over his shoulder. Liam cried out, grabbing and hanging on the man's arm, but her captor shook him off as he hefted Sarah down the boat dock then boarded a thin plank connecting the dock with the speedboat.

"Mommy!"

"Run, Liam! Run," she cried as he backed up on the dock, his sweet, beloved face furrowed with indecision. "Find a man with a black dog. That's Uncle Tucker and Onyx—*oof*!"

Her captor staggered onto the boat, then tossed her down. She slammed onto the damp floor, rolling over a set of orange life jackets. Her world teetered as the small boat wavered from their combined weight and all the movement.

Sarah's chest rose and fell as the horizon spread out in murky shades of gray. Stars dotted her vision. If she stayed on the boat, how would Tucker find her? The lake was huge, and the forest spread thousands of acres across Northwestern Pennsylvania.

"Say goodbye to your son." The man kicked the plank away, and Sarah cried out, attempting to stand on the wobbling watercraft.

"No!" She rose to find Liam had done what she said. He had retreated on the dock, but now turned to watch her. "Look for the black dog!"

He wiped his tear-stained face, and her heart wrenched at having to leave him again so soon.

"Remember what Mommy's really good at?" Then she did the zipping-her-lips motion so he wouldn't say it out loud. Liam nodded, fisting his little hands at his sides.

"Give me a break." Her captor shoved her back down to the floor, then started the engine. It sputtered and groaned, coughing up smoke, then he steered it away from the wood structure and out into the open water.

God, help me please, she prayed as the boat floundered farther into the lake, until they were a few hundred feet from the dock. *I need You, Lord.*

The man stood a couple feet away, engrossed with trying to steer while messing with a paper map he unfolded. She had to go now, before it was too late.

Sarah ignored all the warnings in her brain and climbed on the edge of the boat. She dove, hands poised above her head, straight into the lake. Icy pinpricks speared her muscles as she went under, and shock clenched her lungs as the biting-cold water closed over her. She surfaced and relied on instinct in the near dark. Listening for the grumbling motor, she swam freestyle through the dark water, away from the boat.

Back to her son.

A shout from the shoreline grabbed her attention. *Tucker?* She slowed and lifted her head, wiping the water from her eyes. He sprinted along the dock, up to the edge. He had Liam.

Relief choked her, and she resumed swimming, her tears of joy a baptism of gratitude in the lake.

Thank You, Lord.

She stroked hard and fast, kicking her legs, lowering her face into the water and lifting it every five strokes or so to breathe. *Hurry.* The bitter chill of the water was creeping into her muscles, making them sluggish and heavy. Unresponsive.

"Mom! Over here!"

Liam's little voice cheered her on, but the cold fought against her. Weighed her down, soaking deeper into her numbing skin.

Please, God. I'm almost there.

"Lord in Heaven, protect her." Tucker paced the dock as Sarah glided through the lake. How cold was the water this time of year? Forties? Fifties? They'd had a mild winter so far, but the water temps were still below safe for human activity.

Liam sat with a paramedic on the shoreline, wrapped in a blanket as they checked his vitals. Tucker had told Onyx to stay, and the dog stood sentinel beside Liam, enjoying the boy's little hands running through his fur.

Tucker called over to the paramedics and Heath.

"We're going to need blankets. Jackets. Anything. Get an ambulance down here, now!" His earpiece hung partially out of his ear after the fight with the gunman, who now sat bleeding and handcuffed. Tucker couldn't take his eyes off Sarah as she stroked back toward the dock.

Brave move, jumping off that boat, but she only had a couple of minutes before the cold water would immobilize her. His heart slammed into his ribs. Then she'd drown.

Footsteps alerted him to Heath's presence. He had arrived shortly after Tucker and Onyx had wrestled the shooter to the ground outside the dummy cabin. Tucker had handcuffed the suspect, absently noted some type of pain on his side but ignored it as Onyx tracked Sarah, Liam, and their captor to the boat dock.

The other rangers had checked the area since the kidnapping, but they did so on a fairly predictable rotation. Usually early morning and late afternoon. The suspects must have figured out a spot to hide the boat further down the shoreline while the ranger drove through the grounds.

"Uh, Tuck, you're bleeding." Heath jogged up beside him. "What happened?"

He kept his eyes on Sarah. "It's nothing. Happened by the cabin."

"Porter, get an EMT down here," Heath called out, then addressed Tucker. "How did the suspects get the boat this time of year?"

"Must've brought it along or stolen it." Tucker struggled to find the right words as his mind fogged over. "Will have to check…local marinas."

"Tucker, what's wrong? Whoa, you've been stabbed. Porter, get someone down here *now*."

Moments later two EMTs scurried down the boat dock toward Tucker.

"Who's wounded?" a dark-haired man asked.

Heath pointed to Tucker.

Tucker waved them away, surprised at how tiring just moving his arms was. Sarah was closer now, only twenty feet or so out.

"Mommy!" Liam shouted, perched at the water's edge. Onyx barked, warning him to stay back.

Sarah was almost there. *She's pretty amazing.* Had he said that out loud? And why were those stars twinkling closer? Onyx yelped at him from the shoreline beside Liam.

"Tuck, you better sit. You look paler than an onion. Can we get a bandage on him—now, please?"

Tucker ignored his friend, his focus still on Sarah. She'd swum up to the shoreline, then clambered onto the land, her body violently shaking.

"Make sure...she has blankets." Tucker's voice sounded faraway. Why were the trees closing in?

Heath shouted something about a stretcher.

Tucker cocked his head, partly because he couldn't hear well and partly because his head felt too heavy for his neck all the sudden. Two large hands gripped his upper arms, and then he was pushed down. Why was everything moving?

"Where's...Sarah?"

"She's onshore now. The EMTs are with her. *Sit*, man. You're shakier than a palm tree in a hurricane."

Heath's voice. Suddenly, his vision tunneled, and the world turned dark. The last sensation he felt was a hand catching his head before it hit the wood, and his last coherent thought was a prayer. Sarah and Liam, finally together.

Thank You, God.

SIXTEEN

Sarah was past the point of cold. Past the point of exhaustion. She'd probably only swam a thousand yards, which was an easy practice day for her and the Master's team she coached, but her arms and legs felt thick and clumsy, her fingers immobile. Damp, icy hair clung to her neck and cheeks, and she shivered so hard she could barely stand.

But Liam was okay. She had her son back.

Thank You, Lord. Thank You for helping me have faith.

She scrambled up the cool mud edging the lake on her hands and knees, then Liam jumped into her soaking arms, supergluing himself to her neck. She hated to get him wet, but she wouldn't move. Would never forget the feeling of finally holding him again, their hearts beating together.

"That was a bold move, jumping off the boat."

She lifted her head. Heath stood behind her, gripping a blanket. He set it around her and Liam then stepped back. Two men flanked him, wearing uniforms. Paramedics? She wriggled her fingers, which felt strangely heavy, like her toes.

"I had to get away." She peered past him. "Where's Tucker?"

Movement to her left caught her attention. Onyx trotted alongside a stretcher. A man's arm lay limply to one side, nearly touching the stretcher wheels. *Tucker?*

She stood up, then almost collapsed from the extra weight

of her son and from her legs not working correctly. "Is that Tucker? What happened?"

Heath supported her elbow to keep her steady. "He was stabbed during his altercation with suspect two. He's on his way to the hospital. Are you injured?"

"No, just cold and exhausted." Her heart flip-flopped. "Is he badly hurt?"

"I can't say for sure. Let's get your vitals so you and Liam can get warmed up." The paramedics led them up to a set of small boulders, asked them to sit, then readjusted the huge blanket Heath threw over them to keep in their body heat. Liam pressed against her, as close as he could be without climbing inside like he'd been before he was born. Her throat thickened at the memories, and she lifted him onto her lap to cuddle.

"I love you so much, baby. Thank the Lord you're back with me."

"I love you too, Mommy. Did God save me?"

"He sure did. And your Uncle Tucker. Plus all these brave police officers." A thought struck. "Heath," she called out. "Did you get the other kidnapper?"

"Yes, Onyx and Tucker subdued the shooter. We're going to take Tucker on the first ambulance and the shooter on the other. If you're all clear, you two will ride back into town with me."

Two hours later, after a hot shower, a change of clothes and a warm cup of chicken noodle soup, Sarah and Liam sat in Tucker's hospital room. She and Liam had spoken to Heath while Tucker was in surgery, and they'd given their statements.

The kidnapper who'd forced them to the boat dock was still on the loose, but authorities were swarming Allegheny National Forest. It was only a matter of time before their captor was caught.

The investigation wasn't over, but as far as she was concerned, things in her life were much better. She couldn't stop looking at Liam. His spiky hair and freckles, the soft blue of his eyes. Like his father's. Her chest constricted. Tanner had hurt her deeply, but he had also given her the best gift of her life—Liam. It would be a long process to forgive her deceased husband and trust again, but right now anything felt possible.

She gazed down at Tucker, still asleep after receiving stitches and being given a strong anti-pain medication.

The door creaked open, and Molly and Eli stepped into the room. Eli's adorable little daughter, Skylar, peeked out from between them, her brown curls covering one eye.

"Mom, there's a girl hiding there." Liam pointed.

"Hi, Skylar." She gently pushed down his arm then waved. "This is Liam."

Liam, being an adaptable child and bouncing back after the trauma he'd experienced the last three days, promptly stood up and skipped over to her. He waved. "Hi, I'm Liam."

"I'm Skylar," Eli's daughter whispered back, pushing out from between Molly's and Eli's legs. "Mr. Meow is your cat?"

"Yes, he is my cat. Did you get to pet him too? I love petting him."

"Me too. He's really soft and his tummy makes funny noises."

"That's called purring," Liam told her matter-of-factly. "Cats do that when they're happy."

Sarah giggled at their exchange, then met Eli's and Molly's eyes.

"How's our hero?" Eli asked, his gravelly voice familiar and endearing after Sarah had heard him over the earpiece several times earlier today.

"Still resting." Sarah turned back to Tucker. "The doctor said he needed a dozen stitches, and he'll have to be on an antibiotic for a week to make sure there's no infection." His dark eyelashes rested against his cheeks, and several small freckles dotted his strong nose. He and Tanner shared a few similarities in appearance, but overall, she was grateful they were physically different.

Not to mention a bit scared at how strong her feelings were for this compassionate, protective man.

"Sarah, if you want, we could bring Liam down to the cafeteria to grab lunch?" Molly asked.

She turned and found Molly watching her with a slightly speculative grin. Sarah's stomach twisted. Were her thoughts—no, her feelings—toward Tucker that obvious?

Her husband just died. *Sure, he cheated on you and caught you up in this dangerous plot, but it's too soon. Isn't Tucker still pining for someone else? He's probably not interested, so don't even go there.*

"Actually, if it's okay, I'll go along too." She rose.

Warm, strong fingers shot out, clasping her wrist.

"Don't...leave."

Her knees almost buckled. "You're awake."

Eli stepped over to Tucker's hospital bed. "Hey, man. When you're ready, I have some items I want to go over with you about the investigation."

"Can I have a few minutes with Sarah, first?"

Eli nodded, then Sarah turned to Liam. "Would you like something other than soup to eat? I heard they have grilled cheese downstairs in the cafeteria. Probably chips too."

Liam's eyes brightened, and he pretended to eat a huge, invisible sandwich then rubbed his tummy. Molly and Skylar laughed at his silliness, then Molly guided the two children toward the door. "We'll watch over him. See you in twenty minutes or so."

"Be good, Liam. Thanks, Molly." Then she turned to

Tucker, who was watching them through heavily lidded eyes. Seconds later the door closed, and they were alone.

A dozen thoughts wound through her mind, but only one made sense. "I have Liam back." Tears threatened—happier ones, at least. "Thank you." She leaned forward, pressing a brief kiss to his cheek, then pulled away quickly. "How are you feeling?"

"Better now that you're not...in the middle of that lake."

She clucked her tongue. "The boat was only a few hundred yards out when I jumped off."

"I would've turned into an ice cube and drowned," he croaked, and she handed him a cup with water, helping him drink for several seconds. Once she set it down, he lay his head back on the pillow. "I felt so helpless because I couldn't save you."

"I'm starting to think that's when God works best."

He tilted his head, and a slow, sweet smile broke over his face. "How so?"

"When we can't do something on our own and we need His strength," she spoke reverently, realizing how much she believed the words. It had taken a horrible situation—her son's abduction and their lives on the line—to realize it was true.

Tucker settled one of his hands over hers, and their fingers twined together. Her throat burned from the protective, tender gesture.

"I was cheering for you again, like I did when you were in the Olympics."

"Except this time, it was more important than any Games."

"*Much* more important. Speaking of, Liam is okay? He's not hurt?"

"He was hungry, but he's always hungry," she chuckled. "He had a couple superficial cuts but that's all."

"What a relief and an answered prayer. Sarah," he hesitated. "We'll need him to testify when this goes to court."

"I just got him back, Tucker. How can we do that to him?" She removed her hand from his. "It's like throwing him back to the wolves."

"The DA will take it easy on him. His eyewitness testimony will be of utmost importance to convict the suspects. Yours too."

"I can't think about that right now."

He looked down at his empty hand, then pulled it back and gingerly crossed his arms over his chest.

Sarah straightened as a memory replayed from earlier at the campgrounds. "There is something one of the men said, right before he took us to the lake. In all the craziness afterward, I forgot to tell Heath. The man said they needed me to get something of Tanner's. And Liam mentioned opening something."

"Huh. That's all he said?"

"That's all I can remember. I'll ask Liam about it when he gets back."

"Do you have any idea what they're talking about?"

"No, but give me time. It's been such a crazy day. Maybe something will come to mind. Just…please be gentle with Liam. He acts like he's fine, but he's not. He knew about Tanner." Her voice cracked. "He overheard them."

"Ah, I'm sorry. We'll take care of Liam during this investigation." Tucker rubbed his eyes. "I just need you and Liam safe. Out of harm's way. The best way to do that is catch the rest of the criminals involved in this. Please know that's why I'm bringing this all up."

She soaked in the sound of his low voice declaring how concerned he was for them. Sadness colored her thoughts as she realized she'd rarely heard the same concern from her husband. He'd loved Liam. But Tanner had been consumed with work, especially the last two years. Her mouth pinched.

And consumed with Leighton, his secretary.

"Sarah, what's wrong?"

Words spilled out before she considered their cost. "Tanner was having an affair. I don't know for how long. It's part of the reason..." She shook her head, then ran her palms down her face. "Another reason I was going into his work the other day, is to give him an ultimatum about our marriage."

"Tanner was a fool." A vein throbbed on his forehead, and his voice was rimmed with anger. "A fool to throw away your heart and your love like that."

His passionate words momentarily silenced her. "I told him he wasn't happy because he was obsessed by the work project. Tried to get him to go on vacation. To spend more time with... us. But all he could think about was whether or not Nuexta would be approved. It was almost like his life depended on it."

"Maybe it did. I hope this investigation proves that he acted out of desperation in this case with the DSU. But the more you've shared, the more I realize Tanner's life consisted of one bad choice after another."

"Yeah," she whispered. *Just like hers.*

"There was one good choice, though." Tucker reached across the space between them and gently lifted her chin so their eyes met. "He chose you as a wife and mother for his child."

She shook her head, struggling to believe it.

"It's true. And the failings of my brother shouldn't be on your shoulders. They rest solely on his. I may be hard of hearing in one ear, but I'm not blind. Tanner was. He had a treasure in his grasp, and he let it go. No, two treasures."

Unbidden words came to her lips, a question lodged in her heart from many years ago. She ignored what Tanner and

Molly had said about the woman Tucker had been pining for all these years and plunged into the abyss.

"Why didn't *you* want me, Tucker?"

He pulled his arm back then sank against the pillows, chaotic emotion storming his face. For several seconds he simply looked at her, then dropped his gaze to the far wall, where his stats and pain level were scrawled in blood red on a white board.

"I did, once." His strong profile held her transfixed. "But you were always Tanner's. Never mine. And he's—he was—my brother. There are lines family doesn't cross, and that's the biggest line of all." His mouth flattened. "Plus, Tanner told me what you said that summer about me."

It was her turn to draw back. "What *I* said? What do you mean?"

"About my hearing loss."

Sarah stood, gripping the back of the chair. "I don't recall saying *anything* to him about your hearing loss." She'd never cared about that and never would. It was part of who Tucker was, and part of why she—

No. Her complicated feelings for Tucker needed to remain a secret.

"Tanner said you were annoyed that I always walked on that one side, and that you had to repeat stuff to me sometimes. He made it sound like it frustrated you."

"That's not true." She steadied herself on the chair. How dare Tanner said that to Tucker. "I never said that about your hearing aid or hearing loss. I couldn't have cared less about that. Why do you think I sought you out at Hersheypark that day?" She blinked furiously because if she didn't, tears of righteous anger would spring to life. "You were my friend, Tucker, and I would've…if you had…never mind." She pivoted and hurried to the door. "I'm going to find Eli and Molly."

He called her name as she slipped into the hall, but she wouldn't turn around. Couldn't let herself ponder what he'd just admitted.

He had a treasure in his grasp, and he let it go.

Tucker thought *she* was a treasure. She couldn't process the idea that he'd once cared for her. But she had been blinded, and it was too late for them.

An hour later, Tucker attempted to focus on Eli as they discussed that morning's events at the campground, but his thoughts kept detouring to Sarah. To their conversation right before she'd high-tailed it out of there.

Had she cared about him like he cared about her? And why had Tanner lied about her criticizing his hearing loss if she hadn't?

Possessiveness. That was why.

"Hey, you want to wait to talk about this?" Eli's voice splintered Tucker's thoughts.

"Sorry, my brain's on other things. Let's keep going."

Eli's knowing smile and raised brows needled Tucker.

"So," Eli continued, flipping through a notebook, "we discovered that Doctors Scientists Underground operates out of three major East coast cities. Philadelphia, Charleston, and Atlanta are their main hubs. We found two contacts in Asia as well. This is big, Tucker. Federal-level big. I've got calls into a colleague in Baltimore I'm working with on this investigation."

Tucker's gut knotted up. The bigger this undercover group was, the more dangerous—and deadly—it was for Sarah and Liam.

"Sarah shared that the man who held them captive mentioned needing her to get to an item or items of Tanner's?"

Tucker nodded confirmation, his mind traveling down that

road. What would they need Sarah for? Were they looking for paperwork, keys, photographs, a flash drive?

Eli continued, "Tanner's computer and phone were scrubbed, and the server at Zeta Pharmaceuticals has been subpoenaed for the investigation. Mark Sousa is still MIA. A background check on him came back pretty clean—two speeding tickets and several trips overseas in the last decade. I believe a cross-state trip to check their house in Fountain View for evidence is in order. Officer Stevens said that other than the file on the DSU, they've found nothing else."

Tucker flipped the sheet off and rotated so he was sitting, his sweat-pant clad legs hanging off the side of the bed. When he stood, the world tilted, and the stitched-up wound on his side caught on fire. He grimaced.

"Take it easy, tough guy."

"I don't have time to take it easy," he grumbled.

Eli closed his notebook and stood too. "What's the hurry?"

"You just said it. We need to go to Fountain View, check out Tanner's home office. I should stop in and see my mom."

"Right. We can plan for that."

"Where's Heath?" Tucker asked.

"With Piper. She had a play this afternoon at school. *A Christmas Carol*, he said. Skylar's there with Molly as well."

"Poor guy. He needs time with his daughter." Heath must be exhausted too.

"Right, so I'd like to go along with you to Fountain View," Eli continued. "I promised Moll I'd be back before Christmas. Two days, max. I checked with my supervisor and I'm good to go. Once you're cleared, let's hit the road. My Baltimore colleague is going to meet us there tomorrow."

The door creaked, and Sarah slid inside with Liam. Seeing them together invigorated him. She held a chirping phone out to Tucker like a white flag.

"This has been buzzing for the last five minutes."

"Thanks." He'd forgotten she'd kept his cell for him since the attack at the campground. Their fingers brushed, and heat shot up his arm. He ignored it and typed in his phone code. Several texts flashed across the screen. Three calls.

Two texts from Dean Harding. He closed his eyes. That name… *His mom's neighbor*. A quick check showed the calls were also from Dean. His muscles bunched as he read the first one.

Tucker, your mom had a medical emergency. She was taken to South Philadelphia Regional and they're running tests. Her sister went too and she asked me to let you know. I stayed with them a little while but I have a shift at the store now. Nell asked me to text your sister in law, Sarah, but I don't have her number. Please give me a call.

A second text read:

I tried to call you but you didn't answer. A police officer came to my door and asked about her. He said your brother was killed? I can't believe it. I'm so sorry.

Dean was a retired high school guidance counselor who lived in the condo beside his mom's. Tucker had forgotten Dean worked part-time at a local grocery store.

"I need to call my mom."

He shot off a text to Dean expressing his thanks for watching out for his mom and Nell, as well as for the condolences, then he pulled up his mom's picture in his contacts. The phone rang eight times, then went to voicemail. He tried again, with the same result. Finally, he called Nell, only to have her phone go straight to voicemail.

Dark thoughts burrowed into his mind like termites in a house foundation. Had the men after Sarah and Liam done something to his mom? Or was this illness a result of the medication Tanner and his team at Zeta Pharmaceuticals had given her?

"What's going on?" Eli asked.

"My mom is in the hospital."

Eli and Sarah regarded him with matching concerned expressions as he explained Dean Harding's texts and Tucker's unanswered calls to his mom.

"I need to go too." Sarah held Liam in front of her, looping her hands around his upper arms. "I want to see her."

Tucker almost argued against it, then he realized Sarah was probably closer to his mom than he was. She was her daughter-in-law. The boundaries fell back into place in his mind…and around his heart. Sarah had been Tanner's wife, not his. Tucker's love for her wouldn't ever be a burden, one that she accepted because of desperate circumstances or gratitude rather than simply her choice to make.

Her choice to give him her heart.

No, he would be available to her from now on, a friend to lean on as she transitioned to being a single mom, but he'd shut down those *what if* thoughts.

Thoughts like how much he cared for—no, loved—her. Thoughts like how Liam deserved a father figure who would love him and take care of him. A father figure who wanted to build LEGO sets together and spend time wrestling and hiking.

Use your head.

He had to focus on this case. On his mom and figuring out what these men were after. Not on following his heart after Sarah Brindley.

SEVENTEEN

Sarah thumbed through social media on her cell, the details blurring together as she and Tucker drove to Fountain View in Heath's SUV. Looking through the brief window into other peoples' lives felt wrong when her own was in such turmoil.

Tucker glanced at his cell, set in a holder on the dashboard. "There's about an hour left."

Eli's unmarked car followed behind, providing an extra set of eyes as they attempted to figure out Tanner's secrets before the dangerous men from the DSU did. They would start at her and Tanner's home.

"Are you okay?" Tucker looked over at her.

She pasted on a waning smile. Even though Liam was safe, even though he was well guarded and happy to be reunited with Mr. Meow, her thoughts kept ping-ponging back to her son.

"He's as safe as can be. Having a blast, I'm sure."

He knew her too well. "I'm grateful Heath and Molly have him, and he can stay there with Piper and Skylar and the Calhouns. And Mr. Meow." Even Onyx was there, though the canine wasn't happy about Tucker leaving him. "I'm glad you'll be able to visit your mom."

Tucker reached his right hand over to gently graze her arm and wrist. The touch was fleeting but helped calm her heart.

He'd finally reached his aunt Nell, who explained that his mom had experienced a drop in blood pressure and passed out. In the process, she had hit her head on a piece of furniture, and the head wound bled profusely.

Thank the Lord she was okay, just under doctor's supervision for the next day or two.

She set her phone on her leg. "What's the plan once we get there?"

"Officer Stevens said he'd meet Eli at the station to give him updates about what they've found, while we stop by your house to check Tanner's office. Stevens said that shouldn't be a problem." Tucker drummed the steering wheel. "After that, we'll visit my mom at the hospital. We can stay at her condo tonight, and then head back to Holloway tomorrow."

"I don't know what to look for in Tanner's office."

"Drew said they went through his office space thoroughly. That's where they found the file with the paperwork about the DSU." He made a thinking sound in his throat. "Did you verify your bank accounts weren't hacked or money wasn't withdrawn or deposited the last couple of days?"

"I checked the accounts as I was leaving Fountain View. Nothing seemed out of the ordinary."

"So, the criminals may not have been after Tanner's money. Hmm. More things to go over with Drew."

Fifty minutes later they pulled down the main street of Fountain View. With a population hovering around five thousand, the small suburb boasted a quaint country feel while still being close to the city. Tucker pulled into a gas station, and moments later, Eli followed. Both men stepped out of their vehicles, and Eli came around to speak to Tucker.

Sarah huddled in the seat, waiting. Liam had been upset about her leaving him, but once he reunited with Mr. Meow in the guest bedroom at Heath's house, he'd calmed down.

They'd decided it was best to keep Mr. Meow in the bedroom for the duration so he and the dogs wouldn't tussle.

Tucker slid back into the SUV. "Eli is getting gas, then meeting Drew at the station. Once they go over a few points about the case, they'll join us at your house."

"Which means we have an hour or so?" The wind howled against the windows, and Tucker closed his door, waved at Eli and started back toward the main road.

Tucker glanced at her. "Which way?"

"Take a right here. It's a mile down this road, then turn left on Brantley Boulevard." She frowned. "You've never been to my—to our house, have you?"

He shook his head slightly as he followed her directions. The small storefronts, dressed up with blinking lights and sparkling Christmas attire, failed to lift her spirits. What would it have been like if Tucker had visited them? While Tanner had mentioned Tucker from time to time, he'd never seemed overly interested in having his twin visit, which had always puzzled her.

Sarah blinked at the roadside as it flashed past. Had her soft spot for Tucker—hidden away for years but undeniable now—been obvious to Tanner? Had her husband been threatened by it?

"A left here?" He pointed at the green sign.

"Yes. It's about one-third of a mile, then a right on Meadowbrook Lane. We're number 115."

She sat silently as they approached her tan-and-blue house, a four-bedroom Colonial.

"No Christmas lights, huh?" Tucker asked as he drove past the house.

"I didn't have time this year. Aren't you stopping?"

He peered in the rearview mirror. "Not yet. I want to park

farther away so the car isn't visible from the house. Precautions."

She lifted the thermos Molly had lent her before they left and downed a few big gulps of water, easing her dry throat and mouth. Why was her heart thundering so much? The police had cordoned off the house, and Drew knew they were here.

Tucker circled around and drove back past the house, finally choosing an empty field at the end of the street to park beside. They exited the vehicle together and headed up the sidewalk, their arms jostling. It was a weekday, with only a few days left before Christmas, and the neighborhood was quiet, no people in sight.

Normally, her street bustled with activity. She shivered. Perhaps the cold front that had come through last night was keeping neighbors inside.

"You should've taken Molly up on the offer of her winter coat."

"She's lent me so much I'm starting to feel like I'm taking advantage."

"She doesn't mind. From what Eli says, she has lots of clothes. Besides, you wouldn't take advantage of someone like that anyway, and you're always appreciative."

"You seem to know me well," she replied, a small smile erasing what felt like a permanent frown from the last few days.

"Do I?"

"I think so. You've seen me at my worst this week." Her light tone faded away, and her chest tightened. "I hope you know me well enough to know I would never criticize you or make fun of you for your hearing loss."

"I believe you. I'm just sorry I believed Tanner." His mouth twisted. "I should've just come to you about it. Except then…" He let the words trail off, shoving a hand through his hair.

"Except then...what?"

"Nothing. Our lives are what they are. You have Liam, he's safe, and that's the most important thing now. That and making sure these criminals are caught and brought to justice."

Disappointment clouded her eyes. What had he been about to say? *Drop it.* "Onyx wasn't too happy about being left behind today."

"I think he has a bit of an attachment issue because his previous handler was killed. Plus, he loves being part of the action. But he reopened that cut during the scuffle yesterday. He may not want to, but he needs to rest and heal."

They neared the front porch, and Tucker withdrew his weapon. "Which door is best to use?"

"We usually went in the garage. Here, I'll put in the code."

She strode ahead of him, toward the small gray keypad on the right side of the double garage door. After tapping in the code, she stepped back as the door creaked open. Inside, Tanner's blue BMW sat deathly still, a reminder that its owner would never drive it out of the garage again.

"Tanner's car?"

"Yes." She shuddered. "I still can't believe he's gone."

"I can't, either." He shook his head. "Past the sadness of it, I mostly feel sorry for him."

They stepped into the garage and neared the door to the house, and Tucker hit the garage door button so the door would descend.

"What do you mean, you feel sorry for him?"

"He had a beautiful, caring wife and a fun and loving son, and he threw it all away. I'm ashamed for him. I loved Tanner, but I didn't respect him and now, knowing what he did to you..." His mouth flattened just before he turned away.

Tucker's strong emotion and defense of her and Liam sank into her skin. His sense of protectiveness toward them was such a balm during this awful time, when she not only grieved Tanner's murder but grieved the death of their marriage before that.

If she was honest with herself, she'd been close to leaving him. He had shown little remorse about the affair, other than blaming it on long work hours and poor judgment and Sarah's indifference to him.

They entered the house on the rush of Tucker's sincere words and her heavy thoughts, and Sarah inhaled sharply. Her normally pristine kitchen was in disarray. A few cabinets sat open, and two of the four kitchen chairs were propped beside the kitchen counter as though Liam had been there, trying to get a cup out of a high cabinet. But he had a stool for that. The blinds were drawn, and shadows mixed with the light gray tile and cabinets added a morose feeling to the room.

Her stomach sank. "I didn't leave it like this. Do you think the police did?"

He pulled out his cell. "I doubt it."

Tucker maneuvered around the mess of her kitchen. Coming here with her but with Tanner gone felt odd. Like he was intruding or breaking some unwritten rule.

Staying in a house with Tanner and Sarah had been the absolute last thing he'd ever wanted to do, so he'd normally found an excuse not to come down to visit. Not that Tanner had invited him very often. Maybe twice over the span of their marriage.

"I think the main area we should consider is Tanner's office." They headed through a narrow hallway toward the living and dining rooms. A large Christmas tree dominated one corner, the branches bright green, lights off and ornaments glittering in the house's low light.

"That looks nice. Did you decorate it together?" Tucker motioned at the tree.

"Liam and I did. Tanner was at work that night."

Tucker grunted in disapproval then moved on, checking each room. Sarah had mentioned Tanner's office was on the first floor, so they made their way toward the opposite side of the house. Three doors opened into a small hallway, and he looked to her for further instructions.

"That's a bathroom. This is our guest bedroom, and that's Tanner's office."

Tucker opened the bathroom door, checked it. Then he did the same to the guest bedroom. Finally, he stood in front of the office and used his foot to push the door open. It swung wide, revealing a medium-sized room with two curtained windows and lots of shelves. Two file cabinets flanked the desk, and a stack of paper sat atop the desk. A small, framed picture of Tanner and Sarah was stuck in one corner—their wedding day—while a larger, square frame held a shot of Sarah with a toddler Liam, alongside Tanner at Niagara Falls.

"I want to check the closet." He pointed.

"Tanner's safe is in there," she noted as he crossed the room. Then he stopped and turned. Sarah met his eyes, hers wide.

"A safe?" Could this be what the men who abducted Liam had wanted opened?

They beelined for the closet, and she opened the bifold doors. A row of fancy dress shirts lined the small space. Men's button-down shirts. A couple pairs of slacks.

"Those are Tanner's dry-cleaned clothes. He kept some of them down here instead of in...our closet."

Tucker pushed the clothes aside to reveal a black steel safe backed up against the closet wall. About five feet high and three feet wide, it took up nearly half the closet.

"How long has he had this?"

She shrugged. "A few years." Then she frowned in thought. "No, about two years. He got it after he and his friend Trey started clay shooting. He bought a couple shotguns and a handgun. With Liam in the house, I said he needed a safe."

Tucker felt along the side of the large metal vault. "Do you know the code?"

"It's Liam's birthday, backward." She touched his upper back as he pushed inside the closet. "Do you think…?"

"I think they wanted you to open this," he finished.

"Why didn't the police do it when they were here?"

"They can issue a warrant and open a safe if they believe there's evidence for the investigation inside. But the police may not have seen it. They probably focused more on his work office since that's the actual crime scene. If you hadn't told me this was in here, I might've missed it too. These clothes cover it well."

Tucker sent off a text to Eli.

Found a safe in Tanner's office closet. Sarah knows the code. Let Officer Stevens know asap.

"You mind opening it?" Tucker backed up.

She stepped forward, leaning into the closet, then typed out the code. The keypad beeped, and she turned the large black handle counterclockwise. With a small sigh, the thick door opened to reveal a bloodred interior.

Tucker's eyes widened. The gleam of two brown-and-black shotguns caught his eye. A small shelf sat near the top right of the safe, with a slim manila folder and another gun, this one small. A handgun.

"Does he keep the bullets in here?"

She looked back at him. "I don't think so, he kept them upstairs in his—" She shrieked, and Tucker had one second to avoid the whistling sound coming toward him.

A powerful whack reverberated through his body, sending him sideways. Pain splintered his nerves as he face-planted on the carpet. *Sarah.* He had to keep her safe. Tucker rose to his knees and punched their attacker's middle, throwing the man off-balance. His knife wound screamed at the rapid movements. A gleaming black weapon materialized, and Tucker jumped up and threw himself in front of her. A resounding *pop* filled the room, and prickling heat spread over his shoulder.

I've been shot.

Stars danced before his eyes, and his mind fought the approaching storm as Sarah's face was swallowed up by darkness. *No.*

EIGHTEEN

Sarah struggled against the man as he dragged her out of her house.

"Get off me!" She threw her elbow back, cracking his cheek. The manila folder under his arm fell to the ground, and he loosened his hold to retrieve it.

So *that's* what they were after. What did Tanner have in that folder?

No time to think. She scrambled away and took off, running on legs that felt like spaghetti across her yard, toward the road.

"Help!" she screamed. A dog barked down the street, but otherwise the porches remained silent, doors shut. Christmas lights winked at her, taunting humanity when there was none.

Tucker had been shot. She'd seen blood—lots of it—before the man had grabbed her.

"Help me!" Why weren't any neighbors home? She shouted it again, then reached for her phone. Where was it? Had it fallen when—

Strong arms wrapped around her, lifting her clear off her feet. The manila folder was gripped in her captor's mouth, muffling his curses. Her phone went flying across the pavement. She wriggled against the tight hold, slamming her head back into him. He was ready this time, avoiding the frantic movement, the folder flapping uselessly.

Something about the man seemed familiar. He was the one who'd dragged them from the cabin. The one who had thrown her on the boat.

"Let me go!" she yelped as he tossed her into the trunk of a car and slammed it shut. Darkness surrounded her, so complete she whimpered and curled into the fetal position.

God, please help me, she prayed as the car jolted into motion. *Please save Tucker.*

Had he sent the text off to Eli or Drew? She shivered as the image of him jumping in front of her filled her mind, then the replay of the gunshot blasting in Tanner's office.

The only way to help Tucker was to get away from this guy. The criminal could have the folder. She didn't care about that. None of it mattered except making sure Tucker was okay.

She closed her eyes and focused on the vehicle's direction. A left. Then a right. They were back on the main road in Fountain View. Several moments later, the driver sped up. The highway. Sarah counted off the turns and tried to keep track of the time, but the constant, jarring motions were too much. When the vehicle finally pulled to a sudden stop, she rolled forward.

Then daylight blinded her as the trunk popped open. She pressed herself deeper inside it, panting as a man stood at the opening.

It was Liam's kidnappers, from the cabin.

"Let's go."

She kicked at him, trying to get a look around. Where were they? She could only make out gray sky behind him and a few bare trees. The rush of traffic sounded far away. Too far away.

"Get out!"

"No." She kicked out again, and the man cursed. "Tell me where I am."

Her abductor roared in frustration, and two truths hit her at once. The deep trunk had given her a way to keep the man's hands off her—he had to contend with her legs, her muscles honed from years of kicking in the pool and running and working out. The second thing she realized was that no matter what, she couldn't let Tucker out of her life again.

God, please help Tucker. Please let him be okay. And get me out of here.

"What are you mumbling to yourself? Don't make me come in there and get you."

He leaned in, and Sarah swung hard with her right leg, aiming for his chest. Her aim was true, and he grunted at the impact. One of his arms swept up and grabbed her ankle just as she pulled her leg back. She kicked with her other foot, hitting him smack in the face.

He growled, gripping her ankle even harder. Lightning shot up her leg, and she cried out as he twisted.

"I will not…go with you!"

"Put your hands in the air!" a voice broke through her struggling, and sirens wailed in the background. The crunch of tires on graveled concrete eased her panicked breath. Police?

Her attacker released her ankle and whipped around, disappearing from her view. Sarah huddled in the back of the trunk for several moments, her body humming with adrenaline.

"Sarah?" A familiar voice. Eli?

She scrambled out of the belly of the big trunk, falling into Eli's arms. He caught her and helped her stay steady until she was able to stand on her own.

Across the parking lot to her right, a half dozen uniformed officers dog-piled her attacker. They cuffed him on the ground between the vehicle and a plain one-story building with dark tinted windows and brown double doors. The word *Laundry* was painted above the doors.

To her left—her heart flip-flopped.

Tucker. *Thank You, God.*

A white gauze bandage wrapped his left arm and shoulder. He leaned against Eli's unmarked car, speaking to an EMT with a roll of some kind of medical tape.

"Are you hurt?" Eli scrutinized her.

"No. Just bruised, I think. You guys got here in time." She shook out her legs and wiped her hands down her pants. "How did you find me?"

"Tucker had texted me, and we were on our way over. We must've just missed you by a couple of minutes. Tucker said he saw a black sedan drive away, and Officer Stevens found an email for a paid invoice to this building. The business is called Medical Transcripts, but the signage read *Laundry*, so they investigated that incongruity a little further."

"We think it's a cover for the DSU." Tucker ambled over, moving slowly, his gaze caught on hers.

Her eyes roved over him. *Thank You, Lord.* "You were shot."

"The bullet grazed my upper arm." He lifted it with a grimace. "But it didn't hurt my legs. I crawled to the front window in the office and saw you giving your kidnapper a run for his money." His forehead wrinkled. "You weren't hurt?"

"I don't think so." She held out her arms. "Just a couple scratches. I'm... I was so worried about *you*."

"I'll live to see another day." He gave her a crooked grin.

"You better." She remembered what he said when they were decorating Heath's Christmas tree, that he couldn't lose her again. The truth was *she* couldn't lose *him*. "Are you going to the hospital?"

"Yeah. I rode over in the ambulance. The EMTs cleared me to follow Eli and the other officers here. I had to see you first. Make sure you were okay."

Drew trotted over.

"Find anything inside?" Tucker asked.

"My men seized all the electronics. There are a lot. Get this. This building is fronted as a laundromat, but no clothes. No washing machines or dryers. Instead we found a storeroom with several boxes of medication and vaccines.

"And—" Drew's brows shot up "—Mark Sousa apparently has been inside here since Tanner's murder. He has a passport on him and two suitcases. Looks like he was holing up until he found an opportunity to leave the country. At this point, it appears Alexander Drake wasn't a part of this DSU group." Drew smiled wearily at Sarah. "I'm glad you're okay. Amy wants to see you before you head back to Holloway."

"Thanks, Drew." She tilted her head. "What makes you think I'm heading back there?"

"Well, number one, Agent Buchanan said Liam is still there. And two..." His mouth quirked. "I have a feeling you're wanted there." Then he winked at Tucker, turned and walked away.

"I'll be back shortly." Eli joined Drew, leaving them alone.

She mashed her lips together and dared a glance at Tucker. His soft blue eyes bore into hers, and it felt like they were the only two people standing in the swarmed parking lot.

It took all her self-control not to launch into his arms. Partly because he was wounded and she didn't want to hurt him, but also because...her heart felt like it was on the line.

She loved him. Not just because he was her dear friend. Not just because he protected her and deeply cared about others in such an unselfish way. Not just because she knew beyond a shadow of a doubt that he valued her and would never betray her.

But because he reminded her how much God loved her, and she knew he would always point her back to Him.

"You took a bullet for me." She couldn't wrap her mind around it.

"You're worth it." He stepped closer, but it didn't feel close enough.

The wintry wind blew in, wreaking havoc on her loose hair. It swished across her face as she looked into his eyes. "I wish I could do a rewind on this. On...us."

"I do too sometimes." He reached out with his good arm and gently tucked the stubborn strand behind her ear. "But our lives played out the way God intended, and He brought us to this point together. As much as I wish I could've changed... things between us years ago, that's all in the past. We're here now. Together."

She worked up a small smile. *Together.*

He continued. "We'll get through Tanner's memorial service, help Liam and you—and my mom—grieve. Then we'll wrap up this investigation and the court case. And I'll be there every step of the way."

"What about..." She stopped as a tremble overtook her. It felt like she was standing on the edge of a steep cliff, but below shimmered a beautiful blue lake the exact color of Tucker's eyes. And she knew the lake was deep, so deep, and safe.

She'd tested it, tried it. Found it true and faithful.

"What about *after* all that?"

He linked their hands, then leaned in to press a soft kiss to her cheek. His lips lingered for a moment, warming her clear through. Then he drew back.

"After that will be your choice." He pressed their clasped hands tighter, then brought them to his heart. "I'm not going anywhere."

"Together," she repeated, looking into his eyes. The word

sounded sure and comforting, but not as comforting as this man being part of her and Liam's future.

He grinned that slow, wide smile, and then she stepped into his embrace. *Together.*

EPILOGUE

Tucker stood in Sarah and Tanner's house, keeping one eye on Liam as she finished up with the home inspector and one eye on Onyx, lounging near the front door. Onyx and Mr. Meow had formed a funny bond, one of playful acceptance. Every now and then they chased each other, the cat batting the dog with a well-timed paw while the dog bowed on his front legs, rump in the air, begging for another romp.

The rooms of the large house were bare now, some of the furniture sold and the rest moved days ago to the cottage along the Allegheny River where she and Liam would live.

"Uncle Tuck, look at Mr. Meow!" Liam crawled past on all fours, the large gray cat standing on his back, tip of his tail flickering, looking for all the world like a feline jockey riding a little boy-horse. Onyx joined in, circling them and yipping.

"Liam, be careful," Sarah called out as she organized the paperwork. She walked the inspector to the door, thanked him and then turned to Tucker.

He met her in the entryway as Liam bounded up the stairs nearby, Onyx tailing them until Mr. Meow suddenly became a cat again and stopped to clean himself.

"Any second thoughts?" Tucker lowered his voice, the urge to pull her into his arms overwhelming. During the four months since Tanner's death, he had offered Sarah friendship, a listening ear, a shoulder to cry on, and an extra set of hands with whatever she and Liam needed as they grieved and decided their next steps in life. In turn, she'd let him talk out his complicated relationship with his deceased twin, stroking his arm and wiping his tears. Understanding.

It was still early. Still shocking to think that Tanner was gone. But the blessings abounded like the spring flowers outside. The group that had come after Sarah, Doctors Scientists Underground, had been gutted from the inside out. Mark Sousa had been identified as the head, and once he was caught at the warehouse where Sarah had been taken that day in December, the organization unraveled quickly. From all accounts, Tanner had been pulled into the group unwillingly, and when he'd tried to leave it, his life was threatened. He'd compiled a list of all the names of each member of the DSU—forty-three in total—and each of the transactions from the last several years. He had then printed the information and stored it inside the safe, presumably to be used as blackmail against Mark Sousa and members of the group.

There'd been a huge undercover operation to arrest those involved, and Officer Stevens was working closely with Philly FBI and the CIA to close the case.

Tucker had never been so relieved to return to work with Onyx in the forest. But he'd missed Sarah. Wondered what their future held. His mom had moved in with Sarah temporarily, and her health had improved enough so that she, Sarah and Liam had come to Holloway for a couple of visits. He'd also visited Sarah and Liam, trying to fill in for his brother while also telling his nephew as many of the good memories as he could about Tanner.

Sarah had secured a job at the Holloway YMCA teaching swim lessons and had reached out to the high school to see if they needed help with their swim team. The training facility in Erie was also a possibility, and he was praying they grabbed her up. It was a bit of a drive, but he'd be there to help with Liam. His mom was moving back, too, and they'd all pitch in.

"How much work is left on your kitchen?" Tucker asked.

"The cabinets are being installed today then the floors after that. Maybe a few more days?"

Sarah had used a small portion of Tanner's life insurance policy to remodel the cottage kitchen; install new, secure windows and doors and replace the flooring as well as paint, though they'd done that themselves.

A flush of heat climbed Tucker's neck. The day they'd painted the cottage together... He swallowed. She'd been an efficient but fast painter, flicking it over him several times accidentally as they covered the small bathroom with a second coat of "camel's fur." For revenge, he had dotted her cheeks with his paintbrush, then enjoyed the view with a triumphant grin. But she'd shocked his socks off by kissing him, smearing those paint spots on his cheeks in the process.

Not that he'd noticed. He had only been able to focus on her soft lips on his and how she fit so well in his arms, even so fleetingly, before she'd backed up and said, "Oops," with a grin.

Tucker rubbed his neck as he looked around.

"Any second thoughts about moving to Holloway? Or... anything else?" She had his heart, completely and forever, but he didn't want that to push her into decisions she wasn't ready for.

Sarah set the paperwork down, her pensive gaze running over the house she and Tanner had lived in since Liam was little. A myriad of emotions crossed her face—sadness, grief. Nostalgia. When she finally looked at him, her eyes were soft. Hopeful.

"None at all."

Then she leaned in and kissed him, and he forgot everything except the treasure in his arms and the future they shared.

* * * * *

*If you liked this story from Kerry Johnson,
check out her previous
Love Inspired Suspense books,*

*Snowstorm Sabotage
Tunnel Creek Ambush
Christmas Forest Ambush
Hidden Mountain Secrets
Hunted in the Forest*

*Available now from Love Inspired Suspense!
Find more great reads at www.LoveInspired.com.*

Dear Reader,

Thank you for reading Abducted in the Woods! Sarah, Tucker and Liam experienced a terrible trial in Allegheny National Forest during the Christmas season, and it was a joy to finally write their hard-fought happily-ever-after.

Christmas is the season of hope. After all, God sent His son to earth as a gift for all mankind, and Jesus provides hope for forgiveness of sin and of new beginnings. If you struggle with past mistakes as Sarah did, I pray you remember that Jesus—

Immanuel, God with us—is ready to offer you the gift of forgiveness and grace. He loves you so much.

I enjoy staying in touch with readers! Look for me on Facebook (Kerry Johnson Author), Instagram, or on my website, www.kerryjohnsonbooks.com, where you can sign up for my quarterly newsletter. God bless you and keep you.

Fondly,
Kerry Johnson

Get up to 4 Free Books!

We'll send you 2 free books from each series you try
PLUS a free Mystery Gift.

FREE Value Over **$25**

Both the **Love Inspired®** and **Love Inspired® Suspense** series feature compelling novels filled with inspirational romance, faith, forgiveness and hope.

YES! Please send me 2 FREE novels from the Love Inspired or Love Inspired Suspense series and my FREE gift (gift is worth about $10 retail). After receiving them, if I don't wish to receive any more books, I can return the shipping statement marked "cancel." If I don't cancel, I will receive 6 brand-new Love Inspired Larger-Print books or Love Inspired Suspense Larger-Print books every month and be billed just $7.19 each in the U.S. or $7.99 each in Canada. That is a savings of 20% off the cover price. It's quite a bargain! Shipping and handling is just 50¢ per book in the U.S. and $1.25 per book in Canada.* I understand that accepting the 2 free books and gift places me under no obligation to buy anything. I can always return a shipment and cancel at any time by calling the number below. The free books and gift are mine to keep no matter what I decide.

Choose one:
- ☐ **Love Inspired Larger-Print** (122/322 BPA G36Y)
- ☐ **Love Inspired Suspense Larger-Print** (107/307 BPA G36Y)
- ☐ **Or Try Both!** (122/322 & 107/307 BPA G36Z)

Name (please print)

Address   Apt. #

City   State/Province   Zip/Postal Code

Email: Please check this box ☐ if you would like to receive newsletters and promotional emails from Harlequin Enterprises ULC and its affiliates. You can unsubscribe anytime.

Mail to the Harlequin Reader Service:
IN U.S.A.: P.O. Box 1341, Buffalo, NY 14240-8531
IN CANADA: P.O. Box 603, Fort Erie, Ontario L2A 5X3

Want to explore our other series or interested in ebooks? **Visit www.ReaderService.com or call 1-800-873-8635.**

---

*Terms and prices subject to change without notice. Prices do not include sales taxes, which will be charged (if applicable) based on your state or country of residence. Canadian residents will be charged applicable taxes. Offer not valid in Quebec. This offer is limited to one order per household. Books received may not be as shown. Not valid for current subscribers to the Love Inspired or Love Inspired Suspense series. All orders subject to approval. Credit or debit balances in a customer's account(s) may be offset by any other outstanding balance owed by or to the customer. Please allow 4 to 6 weeks for delivery. Offer available while quantities last.

Your Privacy—Your information is being collected by Harlequin Enterprises ULC, operating as Harlequin Reader Service. For a complete summary of the information we collect, how we use this information and to whom it is disclosed, please visit our privacy notice located at https://corporate.harlequin.com/privacy-notice. Notice to California Residents – Under California law, you have specific rights to control and access your data. For more information on these rights and how to exercise them, visit https://corporate.harlequin.com/california-privacy. For additional information for residents of other U.S. states that provide their residents with certain rights with respect to personal data, visit https://corporate.harlequin.com/other-state-residents-privacy-rights/.

LIRLIS25